MONTAINE'S REVENGE

Days before the end of the Civil War, Sergeant Cody Montaine is gunned down and left for dead by a bunch of deserters led by Butte Fresno. He survives the vicious attack, but loses his memory. Taking the name of Lucky Johnson, he sets out to piece his life back together. Periodic recollections lead Cody to the town of Las Vegas, where Fresno has assumed his identity. Will Cody get revenge and so exhume his old life?

DALE GRAHAM

◆

MONTAINE'S REVENGE

Complete and Unabridged

LINFORD
Leicester

First published in Great Britain in 2012 by
Robert Hale Limited
London

First Linford Edition
published 2014
by arrangement with
Robert Hale Limited
London

A catalogue record for this book is available
from the British Library.

ISBN 978–1–4448–1813–0

Published by
F. A. Thorpe (Publishing)
Anstey, Leicestershire

Set by Words & Graphics Ltd.
Anstey, Leicestershire
Printed and bound in Great Britain by
T. J. International Ltd., Padstow, Cornwall

This book is printed on acid-free paper

1

Epitaph Ridge

The date was 7th April, in the year 1865. The time, a little after the noon hour. Only two days remained before the signature of renowned Confederate general Robert Lee would be reluctantly appended to a document indicating the end of hostilities in the American Civil War.

For four long years, the country had been riven by a bloody clash of arms. North and South had fought a bitter conflict which decimated the Confederate states leaving thousands killed and injured on both sides.

But two days can seem like a lifetime for those still engaged in the death-dealing campaign. Nobody on the front line had any understanding of the manner in which history was about to be played out.

Confederate forces of the 6th Georgia Foot were avidly digging in along the raised spit of strategic ground known as Epitaph Ridge.

Once cloaked in a thick mantle of trees, the top of the ridge had been reduced to an ugly patch of shattered stumps. The pounding from Union artillery had been constant for the last three days and nights. A softening up process for the final push that General Ulysses Grant expected would finally end the war.

But Robert E. Lee was not to be so easily beaten.

His dogged, some might say obstinate, resolve to pursue the cause to which he was passionately dedicated continued to drive his actions. Having been relentlessly pushed back into a small pocket of upland country close to Appomatox, Lee had fervently exhorted his officers into believing that victory was still within their grasp.

Epitaph Ridge! A prophetic name indeed.

Here it was that Lee intended to make a final stand with the avowed intention of turning the tide of the war in the South's favour.

He was counting on fresh provisions and ammunition for his blockaded troops. But when the crunch came, the desperately needed supplies were not there. Mere pipe dreams of a defeated cause, just like many other vague promises in recent weeks that had failed to materialize.

Yet still the revered general's officers were prepared to follow him into the face of certain defeat. The jaws of death beckoned.

But not everyone was so instilled with this idealistic zeal.

'Hear that?' The blunt query emerged from between the scowling lips of Private Butte Fresno. The mean-eyed trooper had been digging out a foxhole. Resting on his shovel, he slung a meaningful thumb towards the distant cough of gunfire. 'Them blood-crazy bluebellies must have already launched an attack at the north end of the ridge. By sundown they'll have overrun the whole damned position.'

'What can we do about it, Butte?' whined a small rat-faced dude known as Mingus Charlie. 'Sergeant Montaine'll skin us alive if'n we try to surrender.'

'Ain't no chance of that,' grumbled the third member of the slit trench. Idaho Black was a born pessimist who lived up to his name by always finding some reason to complain. They could be munching on a succulent piece of fried chicken and the critter would claim it was poisoned. 'Them boys'll slit our throats rather than bother with the hassle of prisoners.'

Charlie offered the morose comment a dull nod of accord. Then he scrambled out of the trench. 'Well I'm goin' to the latrine afore crunch time arrives.' He disappeared into the midst of the blackened remnants of the forest.

Time passed slowly. Each renewed burst of gunfire brought the coming battle that much closer to the beleaguered defenders of Epitaph Ridge. Soon they could even pick out the raised voices of the excited attackers. The unearthly clamour sent a tremor of fear down Black's spine.

Fresno stuck his head above the rim of the foxhole and peered around. The next trench was out of sight around a rocky outcrop. Nobody else was anywhere near. Theirs was the final dugout in the line.

The hard-assed jasper scowled. That bastard Montaine had threatened them with dire consequences if they moved an inch from their forward position overlooking the back slope of the ridge. Keep your eyes peeled and your fingers on the trigger, he had said.

'Stuff that,' Fresno muttered under his breath.

An increasing amount of gunfire permeated the smoke-laiden air. And judging by the more pronounced growl, he was right. It was coming closer.

The tough infantryman leapt to his feet.

Again he slung a cautious glance in all directions to ensure they were alone. A nod of satisfaction followed.

It was now or never. Montaine would return soon, and that would be it. They would be stuck here. The blinds would be drawn, sure curtains for them all. After all the fighting they had survived over the last few years, was this how it was going to end? Shot to pieces within sight of the finish line?

Butte Fresno was no coward. He had fought hard for the South. And come through innumerable close shaves in the process. Manassas, Chancellorsville, Antietam, even Gettysburg. He'd survived them all with little more than a few cuts and bruises. Such good luck was certain to run out.

And Fresno was convinced that this was the time.

The South was finished. But not Butte Fresno. No sirree!

'You comin' with me?' he snapped at the cowering form of Idaho Black. 'Or are yuh just gonna skulk in that hole and get filled with yankee lead?'

'What about Montaine?' countered the weasel. 'He'll have our guts if'n we leave our position.'

'Not if'n we ain't around he won't.' Fresno was getting impatient at the delay. He was used to his buddy's gloomy portents, but this was no time for dithering. 'You comin' or not?' he rasped before adding, 'just remember that saying: 'He who runs away, lives to fight another day'.'

Black was more afraid of being left alone to face the enemy than any repercussions from Sergeant Cody Montaine. He leapt out of the hole faster than a coalminer on payday.

'Where are you two varmints sneaking off to?'

The blunt-edged challenge took the deserters completely by surprise.

After receiving his orders regarding defence tactics from the officer-of-the-watch, Montaine had been checking on the other trenches further along the ridge. He knew that Butte Fresno had been stirring up trouble among the men. The sly jasper had a silver tongue; he could easily sway those whose loyalty was wavering, and who were less than eager to face a determined and relentless foe.

Both of the absconders were struck dumb. Even Fresno was lost for words. All he could see was the ugly snout of a Smith & Wesson .38 pointing at his belly. His mouth dropped open.

'I'm waiting for you pair of yellow scum to explain why you're all set to abandon your post. Deserters!' This last accusation was spat out with repellent defiance.

The noncom wagged his pistol, a wary eye holding the duo in a firm grip. The sharp crack of small-arms fire mingled with the throaty roar of cannon shells. Montaine had to shout to make himself heard above the growing cacophany of approaching battle.

'Desertion in the face of the enemy is a terminal offence, not to mention being the action of cowards. I'd be doing my duty to shoot you both down here and now. But the company needs all the men it can muster.' Montaine spat a lump of chewing baccy at the feet of the troopers. 'Even down to rats like you. Now get back in that hole where you belong.'

'We ain't stupid, Montaine.'

The cutting rejoinder had come from behind the sergeant. Montaine stiffened. Now it was his turn to be caught off guard. He cursed aloud, angry at himself for having forgotten about the absence of the third member of the unsavoury trio.

'This war is finished. The South's finished.' Mingus Charlie coughed out a sneering condemnation. 'Epitaph Ridge ain't gonna be another cemetery like at Gettysburg for us. Any fools that stay deserve all they get.' The hammer of Charlie's Navy Colt snapped back. 'Now drop that hogleg and step away.'

Montaine remained anchored to the spot. Only a slight tension in the chiselled jawline betrayed any of the turmoil that was churning up his guts. All his training, his loyalty to General Lee and the 9th Georgia Foot Regiment screamed at him to swing round and take his chances. Being outwitted by a bunch of cowardly snakes didn't sit well at all.

Time hung over the bleak landscape like a wet blanket. Nobody moved.

Then it happened.

A rumbling gurgle of rage cut through the heavy atmosphere as the noncom made his play. Lean hips swivelled in one fluid move, the .38 lifting.

But he was too late. Mingus and his partners had also been well trained. The Colt pistol blazed fire and lead. Montaine jerked once as the lethal ball ruptured his shoulder blade. He reeled back. Blood poured from the ugly wound as the injured man sank to his knees.

Not one to allow such an opportunity to go begging, Butte Fresno grabbed for his own pistol and loosed two more bullets into the dying body. He didn't wait to check whether the hated noncom was dead.

'Let's get out of here,' he yelled jabbing a raised boot into Montaine's swaying torso. 'It's lucky for us that the bluebellies are close. Far as anybody else is concerned, this critter was shot by them.'

'What about searchin' this guy?' inquired Black. 'I ain't got two cents to rub together. You guys packin' any dough?'

'Only this Confederate rubbish,' concurred Mingus extracting a small roll of notes from the pocket of his tattered grey uniform. He tossed the worthless money into the air. It floated in the low breeze like a flock of pigeons.

'Good thinkin', pard,' Fresno praised his buddy as he quickly frisked the still body of the prone sergeant. 'Here's some real dough.' He smiled tossing the wad to Black. 'And this looks mighty interestin' as well.' He held up an official-looking document boasting an impressive red seal. 'Looks like a deed of inheritance.' He stuffed it into his pocket cocking an ear towards the rapidly advancing sound of the enemy forces. 'We'll study it later once we're in the clear.'

Bending low he scampered away followed by his two sidekicks.

Within seconds, the welcoming embrace of the decimated woodland had swallowed them up. Enemy fire slammed into the nearby rocks ricochetting in all directions. Screams and yells of pain filled the death-dealing air as battle was engaged. The deserters had escaped in the nick of time.

The defenders of Epitaph Ridge put up a heroic resistance. But the conclusion was swift and inevitable, just as Butte Fresno had predicted.

Another half hour and the ridge had been overrun by the attacking Union forces. The body of Sergeant Cody Montaine was just one of many littering the battlefield on that grisly afternoon.

* ★ ★

Two days later, the Confederate Army surrendered. The war was over.

It was during this period that the bodies were cleared from the battle-field. Checks were made to determine if any of the fallen troops had survived the assault. Union medical attendants scowered the ridge looking for the tell-tale signs of life.

Being at the far end of Epitaph Ridge, Cody Montaine's platoon was the last position to be reached.

'Nothing here for us,' called one attendant to his partner. 'These poor dudes are all graveyard fodder.' He moved away lighting up a smoke to try and disguise the stench of death that permeated the leaden atmosphere.

Something made him pause. A sixth sense maybe. Or was it something else?

Then he heard it. Low but distinct. A groan. Turning round, he saw a raised arm. His eyes bulged wide: a survivor.

The only one amidst so much carnage. It was a miracle.

'Stretcher! Stretcher!' he yelled. 'Over here, quick.'

2

Overland Stage

The lurching coach was five miles north-west of the Palo Duro relay station in the Texas panhandle. The horses of two of its passengers trailed behind. It had slowed to a steady walk in order to safely cross the broad reach of the Carrizo River. At this time of the year, the river was at its lowest. The Butterfield Overland operated a weekly service between Amarillo and Santa Fe which normally took a week, stopping at various overnight halts. Palo Duro was the first.

The next stop was Cimarron in New Mexico.

Only one new passenger had joined at the station when the horses were being changed for the next part of the journey.

Nattily dressed, the jasper sported a garish silk vest beneath a green velvet jacket. A tall beaver-skin hat rested atop an untidy thatch of black hair. Already the guy was displaying his profession by playing patience on the upturned bottom of his valise. Shifty eyes flitted between the other passengers. No doubt he hoped to entice them to join him in a proper game at the next stopover.

Apart from the usual greetings when they had boarded the coach at the start of the journey, nobody had spoken. Conversation languished as the early morning heat began to make its presence felt.

Opposite the tinhorn in stark contrast, sat a thin-faced jasper. He was clad in a black suit and matching hat which, likewise, advertised his calling. The Reverend Amos Farrow was avidly studying his Bible. Perhaps he was preparing a sermon on the evils of gambling.

This thought was passing through the

16

mind of a rather slight young woman sitting on his left. Miss Felicity Harper felt rather uncomfortable surrounded by all these men. Demure, somewhat strait-laced, she was nonetheless an attractive girl with bright azure eyes, accentuated by wavy blonde hair that rippled like a windblown cornfield.

She had tried unsuccessfully to avoid catching the eyes of the other passengers, but trapped in such close proximity, it had proved to be an impossibility.

Not that the male passengers were complaining. The comely Miss Harper offered a far more enticing sight than the bleakly endless wilderness of sagebrush, sand and mesquite.

'You travelling far, miss?'

The young fellow sitting on the far side by the window was the first to break the silence. Cal Mason offered her a friendly, open smile. Faded range garb and long legs swathed in leather chaps told everyone that he was a cowboy, no doubt returning to his home ranch following a cattle drive to the nearest railhead.

'I intend setting down at Las Vegas in New Mexico territory,' replied the girl, curtly. Her eyes lowered discreetly. A rather conservative pout of her smooth lips was meant to convey a modest and restrained persona. However, it occasioned the opposite effect.

Although it was the disclosure of her destination that caused most interest. And not of a positive kind. Widening eyes received the news with barely suppressed doubt. Even the natural poker face of the gambler slipped momentarily. Numerous indrawn sighs of breath informed the girl that Las Vegas might not be the utopian dream she was anticipating.

For some moments, a pregnant silence descended over the unlikely conclave of travellers. Nobody was willing to question the girl as to her motives for choosing such a den of iniquity.

It was the most enigmatic of the group who finally voiced the question all the others had wanted to ask. Tall, with a weathered face that gave an impression of strength and gravitas, he was a man of few words. But unlike the other passengers, his appearance afforded no outward clues as to a particular professional leaning.

Although if they had glanced towards the tooled-leather gunbelt with its well-oiled Remington six-shooter, this omission might well have been rectified. Thus far his comments had been little more than monosyllabic, so it came about that his query held a firm measure of bewitching allure.

'Might I be so bold as to inquire, miss, what business a lady of obvious refinement has in a dive like Las Vegas?'

The lady in question instantly picked up on the salient and rather blunt question. Her poignant gaze narrowed.

'And why should I not be going there? Cannot a citizen travel where he . . . or she pleases?'

The cutting retort elicited a teasingly vague half-smile from the mysterious stranger.

'Indeed so, miss.'

He paused to light up a cigar. A plume of blue smoke dribbled from between pursed lips, filtering out through the open window of the lurching coach. The mahogany brown eyes, though hard as granite, contained a hint of blithe levity. But only for a moment. The words that followed held a prophetic warning that only a fool would ignore.

And Miss Felicity Harper was certainly no moon-calf.

'What these gentlemen are implying by their somewhat ornery expressions' — a leery eye flashed across the other passengers — 'is that Las Vegas has a less than, shall we say, settled reputation.'

That was the point when the gambler butted in with a throaty guffaw. It was followed by a curt down-to-earth addendum.

'What this guy is trying to say, madam, is that the town is a real hell's-a-poppin' berg, full of hardcases and no place for a lady of' — Kirk Diamond tilted his hat in a mock display of deference as the agile brain searched for the right word — 'a lady of elegance and culture.'

'I hear tell Doc Holliday has taken up residence in the Red Dragon saloon,' interjected the young cowpoke excitedly. 'I can't wait to get an eyeful of that guy.'

Miss Harper puffed up her shoulders, nose firmly pointing skywards before she deigned to make a reply.

'If you must know,' she said with haughty disdain, 'I am going to Las Vegas to join my fiancé. We are to be married in the near future.' Holding up her hands, she indicated adamantly that this was her last word on the matter. 'I do not wish to discuss it any further, thank you.' Then, arms folded across her ample bosom, she proceeded to take an inordinate interest in the barren landscape offered by the Texas panhandle.

It was some time later as the stage coach was approaching the territorial border with New Mexico that her starchy demeanour softened.

There was no denying that the unfathomable stranger intrigued her. She could sense an underlying hint of menace, danger even, beneath the soft-spoken exterior. It was a woman's intuition. And Miss Harper was itching to delve beneath the surface.

She drew in a deep breath. 'And what of you, sir?' she said trying unsuccessfully to conceal her inquisitive nature. 'Are you heading that way on business?'

The stranger gave the suggestion a leery smile. His eyes swung to fix this winsome young creature with a wary regard.

'I am a hunter, Miss Harper.'

The girl considered this unexpected news before replying.

'Are you here to shoot buffalo?' She flicked a loose handkerchief at the ever-present swarm of flies that seemed to be paying her more than a casual degree of attention. None of the other passengers appeared to be thus inconvenienced. 'I hear that the army at Fort Union is expanding.'

The terse announcement was met with a derisive scoff from the gambler.

'He ain't no buffalo skinner, that's for darned sure.' Diamond spat the caustic retort out with a derisive snort. A cold glare challenged the man opposite to deny the assertion. 'I'd bet a royal flush that this guy is after two-legged prey. And I ain't talkin' about monkeys, neither.'

It took a moment for the significance of the tinhorn's claim to sink in.

'You mean that he's a — '

'You said it, sister.' The cardsharp's taunting smirk widened into a full blown grin. 'He's a bounty hunter.'

Miss Harper's mouth opened in shocked surprise.

'Is this true, sir?'

The man merely shrugged. He wasn't ashamed of the manner by which he earned a living. And he didn't figure he had to explain himself to anybody. Outlaws and killers who had acquired a price on their heads were a danger to society. Hauling such riff-raff in was doing everybody a big favour.

By its very nature, manhunting trod a fine line, often stepping across ill-defined legal boundaries to achieve its ends. Folks ought to appreciate the tough job he was doing instead of looking down their imperious noses at guys like him.

Some certainly did, crossing the street rather than be tainted by the aura such men carried with them. It was a lonely life. And only the best survived. Lucky Johnson was one such aficionado.

His silence spoke volumes. There was no need for explanations, excuses. He just stared ahead, thinking. The glazed demeanour appeared to be fixed on some indeterminate point at a different time, a different place.

How had he got himself involved in such a precarious way of life?

3

Enter Lucky Johnson

After being dragged back from the brink at Appomatox, it had taken more than a year for Cody Montaine to fully recover from the attempt on his life. His general health and strength were back to normal. Everything should have been hunky dory. There was only one problem.

He was suffering from amnesia.

Much of what had occurred on Epitaph Ridge was a blank canvas. He couldn't even remember his name. The doctors had assured him that given time, and patience, everything should return. But eight years down the line, there were many vital gaps still remaining to be filled.

He had decided to call himself Lucky Johnson due to the fact that it was a miracle he had survived. John was the name of the corpseman who had plucked him from the jaws of death.

Following his release from hospital, Lucky had drifted west. He sensed that working the land was in his blood. So what better way to start his new life than on one of the burgeoning cattle spreads down in Texas. He joined an outfit called the Bowline and spent the next two years pushing herds of longhorns up the trail to Abilene.

These drives later veered towards Ellsworth and other cattle towns once the railroad began moving further west.

It was after picking up his final payout in Hayes City that events were conspiring to change his life thereafter.

For once, Lucky Johnson had not joined his buddies at the end-of-trail celebration. Such blowouts inevitably led to an over-indulgence of hard liquor. Not to mention sore heads the next day.

Some of the crew always ended up in the hoosegow handing over a hefty wedge of their hard-earned dough to the local tinstar in fines. Shooting up a saloon was a favourite pastime in which Lucky had indulged on one occasion only. He had learned his lesson the hard way. Not any more.

More important, however, he had been offered the job of leading hand by his boss, Preacher Henry Masden.

Masden was not a real cleric, but his puritanical ways were administered with religious zeal. He was a tartar when it came to the demon drink. Nary a drop was allowed on the three month drive up from Texas. Anyone caught with a bottle in his possession was instantly sent packing. It was one reason why the crew went a bit wild once they hit town.

To Lucky Johnson, the rancher's offer meant an extra five bucks a month in his pay packet. And he knew that any hint of inappropriate behaviour would most certainly scotch his promotion prospects.

So it was that Lucky found himself

wandering back to the rooming house on the edge of Hayes City earlier than usual. It was a fine clear night. He paused to admire the myriad of twinkling stars splayed across the black canvas of night. An owl hooted in the distance.

He rolled a stogie and lit up. Yes indeed, he smiled to himself. Life was looking up. Even if he still couldn't remember much about it.

That's when he saw them.

Three men were lurking in the entrance to a narrow alley on the far side of the street between the premises of a meat purveyor and a saddler. Not unduly suspicious, except for the fact that they had palmed their hand guns. Lucky cast an eye up and down the street. It was empty apart from a single man walking down from the middle of town.

And he was clutching a bag.

The trio had not spotted Lucky. Their whole attention was focused on the approaching victim. Twenty yards to go. The bushwackers tensed, readying themselves for the snatch.

Lucky was in a quandary. What should he do? He could just turn away. After all, it was no business of his. But that was not his way. Just like the three deserters at Epitaph Ridge, he could have got out before the final debacle. But he stayed to do his duty. Then it struck him.

Three men!

That was the first time he had recalled how many had been responsible for trying to kill him. One had shot him from behind, then another had completed the job while he was crippled. Then the memory faded. He could still not remember their names.

He thrust aside the sudden recollection.

Somebody needed help. He stepped down into the street. The weak light cast by a crescent moon was barely enough to see by. But it enabled Lucky to move closer without being seen. The innocent victim was almost at the alley when Lucky voiced a brusque challenge.

'Drop them hoglegs and raise your mitts!'

For a brief instant the bushwackers froze. The object of their attention also stopped. Then they swung towards the danger, guns rising to take out the lone intruder.

Lucky gave them no chance. His six-gun blazed. Orange flame lancing from the barrel of the .36 Navy Colt added a touch of macabre colour to the morbid tableau. Three shots melded to a single lethal blast, each of them finding a different target. The three figures spun round like dancing marionettes as the heavy balls of hot lead struck home.

They all slumped to the ground. Dead.

As the stentorian echo of death faded, the lone figure on the boardwalk swayed clutching an upright post for support.

'You all right, mister?' shouted Lucky.

The guy just stood there, stunned

into shocked immobility.

Lucky blew off the wisp of smoke twining from his gun barrel. He returned the weapon to its crossover holster. Then he stepped across to the shaking form he had just saved from being robbed, and most likely killed.

The guy was sweating. Shaking hands with the Grim Reaper is apt to leave its mark on any man. Yet he still had the nous to hold on to his bag. The supposition being that it had to contain something of great value.

After being led to a handy bench on the sidewalk, the two men found themselves surrounded by a plethora of curious onlookers drawn by the ugly yet mesmeric sound of gunfire.

Mutterings as to the reason for the shooting rustled through the assembled throng like windblown leaves on a tree. The three corpses of the ambushers were hidden by the raised boardwalk.

The explanations for the ambush soon became apparent.

'There's three bodies over here,'

called out one observant bystander.

'Who were they after?' voiced another.

'It's Dandy Vic Solana,' exclaimed a third individual peering at the shaken figure on the bench. 'Them bushwackers musta been after his takings.'

'Had to come sooner or later,' responded the first man. 'Everybody in town knows that on Saturday night he allus takes the saloon's early takings back to his house for safe keeping.'

Lucky now had no reason to ask the victim what had occurred.

'Stand back!' he called waving his arms for space. 'Give Mr Solano a breath of air.'

The saviour of the town's most popular saloon owner received instant compliance. A jasper that can gun down three armed bandits in less time than it takes to shout 'Draw!' deserves a heavy measure of respect.

The crowd pulled back.

'Anybody got a shot of brandy for this guy?' Lucky asked.

A hand clutching a hip flask shot out.

He tipped a hefty measure into Solano's mouth. 'That should bring him back to life.' The comment was issued with a mild chortle.

The hard liquor soon elicited the desired effect. Coughing and spluttering as it slammed home, the saloon owner's slouching body suddenly lurched. His mouthed flapped, dragging in cool air to quench the flames. Glassy eyes bulged. They swung towards the man sitting beside him.

A couple of minutes passed before Dandy Vic was able to croak out a reaction to his recent close encounter with the scytheman. He held out a grateful meaty paw.

'I'm obliged for your timely intervention on my behalf, young man,' opined the saloon owner, quickly recovering his normal dogmatic presence. The tone offered to Lucky Johnson was appreciative of the service shown, if rather brusquely delivered. 'Perhaps you will accompany me the rest of the way along the street to my house.' He tapped the leather bag. 'Can't be too careful where this amount of dough is concerned.'

You should have thought about that before leaving the saloon alone, mused Lucky. But he kept the damning conclusion to himself.

Solano pulled out a couple of large Havanas and handed one to Lucky. A brief snap of the fingers saw a lighted match being instantly applied to the expensive cigars.

Lumbering to his feet, Solano adjusted his well-cut suit and tie. Another curt twist of the lip and his fallen hat was deferentially placed in an outstretched hand. Exhibiting a nonchalant flourish, he set the pearl grey Stetson at a jaunty angle atop the thatch of wavy black hair.

'Someone get the undertaker to collect these corpses.' Solano's nose twitched in a dogmatic sniff. 'They make the place look untidy.'

'Sure thing, Mr Solano,' said one fawning toady hurrying away. 'And I'll tell the marshal at the same time.'

Solano responded with a curt nod.

Then he led the way along the street leaving the muttering throng behind to discuss the happening, no doubt over a beer at the Dirty Devil. And why not? It was the best drinking den in town.

Being seen to have displayed fear in the eyes of others did not sit well with a man of Vic Solano's standing in the town. These clear-cut actions, however, had been enough to reassert his status as a leading citizen in Hayes City.

Even though he outwardly exhibited a cool air of being in command of his own destiny, the incident had shaken Solano to the core. He had thought himself invincible, immune to the dangers prevalent in frontier communities. Coming face to face with death had brought him down to earth with a bump.

'Seems I owe you a heap of thanks, mister,' he asserted taking a closer look at the Good Samaritan. And he liked what he saw.

The tough raw-boned profile imbued an aura of stolid reliability. Here was a guy who didn't scare easy, a guy prepared to face down a predator, three in fact, without fear or hesitation.

When the unlikely duo reached Solano's residence at the more prosperous end of town, the businessman invited his protector inside. While the saloon owner deposited the first set of takings in his own personal safe, Lucky was left to admire the opulent surroundings that a successful life could bring.

It was a far cry from punching cows. Never in a million years could a guy in his position ever hope to emulate such a lavish lifestyle.

'Nice, eh?' Solano appeared to have read his visitor's mind. He had already arrived at the correct assumption that Lucky was a humble cowhand. 'Maybe some of this could rub off on you.' He paused to pour his guest a glass of the finest French brandy. 'If'n you've a mind.'

Lucky gave the comment a quizzical frown. He sipped the fine liquor, appreciating its five-star ambience, waiting for the older man to elucidate.

'You handled a dangerous situation tonight with flawless ease,' continued Solano strolling slowly up and down the room. 'Few people could have taken out three desperadoes like you did. And after warning them beforehand. Most jiggers would have refused to get involved in another man's plight.' He fixed a curious eye on the cowboy. 'How come you didn't just turn your back?'

Lucky's response was an oblivious shrug.

'Didn't seem proper to let a bunch of skunks get away with robbing you,' he said, quickly adding, 'I ain't no hero, Mr Solano. Just a simple cowpoke. But I do know right from wrong.'

'Well it's lucky for me you were able and willing to put such a noble attitude into practice, else I'd have been occupying a cold marble slab in the mortuary instead of those critters.' Solano shivered at the recollection. A cold hand clutched at his beating heart. 'I've been a durned fool to reckon nobody would ever challenge me. Arrogant and pig-headed. It's a miracle that it hasn't happened sooner.'

He peered at his guest whose craggy features had split in a cheesy grin. A dark frown soured the saloon owner's handsome face.

'You find that amusing, mister?'

'No! You got me wrong,' exclaimed the cowboy hurriedly. 'It's only that my name's Lucky Johnson. Seems like we're both beholden to a guardian angel for keeping us out of the devil's grasp.'

Solano relaxed, returning the smile. His visitor then proceeded to quickly explain the circumstances of his having acquired the new appellation.

When he finished, Solano considered the account thoughtfully while sipping his drink. Nothing more was said for some minutes while both men smoked and drank, musing on their own parallel situations.

It was Solano who broke the silence.

'How keen are you to get back to Texas?'

The question was blunt and to the point. Again, Lucky eyed the speaker somewhat askance from over the rim of his glass.

'Depends what you have in mind.' His reply was cautious, hesitant. What was the saloon owner getting at? He puffed on the cigar allowing the smoke to trickle from the side of his mouth. 'Although I should tell you that I've just been offered the job of leading hand with the Bowline.'

'And what does that pay?'

'Forty bucks a month and all found.'

Lucky was wondering where all this was leading. He waited for Solano to fill him in.

4

A New Direction

'What if I was to offer you fifty . . . a week to act as my personal bodyguard.' He fixed the cowboy with a sober regard before his wide mouth broke into a loose smirk. 'And all found, naturally.'

Lucky's eyes widened. He had not expected such a generous offer.

'You serious, Mr Solano?'

'Never more so, Lucky.' The big man ceased his pacing and faced the younger man. 'You saved my life. And it's clear as the nose on my face that I've been too darned casual about taking care of my goods. So I need a guy to watch my back. Someone I can trust to look after all my holdings in Hayes, someone who's handy with a gun . . . someone like you.' He paused allowing the proposal to sink in. 'So what d'you say? Is it a deal?'

It was now Lucky's turn to stand up and pace the room. He'd enjoyed his time working for the Bowline, and greatly appreciated the offer from Henry Masden. But there was no denying it was a tough job. And in comparison to Solano's offer, the pay was derisory. This offer would give him a chance to spread his wings, move up in the world and earn some serious dough.

There was really no competition. He stuck out his hand.

'It's a deal, Mr Solano.'

The owner of the Dirty Devil grasped it firmly.

'Glad to hear it,' he said buoyantly. 'And now that we're gonna be working so close together, just call me Vic. Where you bunking down at the moment?'

'Ma Jackson's Rooming House on Elgin Street.'

Solano snorted. 'Go down and shift

your gear up to the Imperial Hotel. Can't have my personal minder sleeping in that flea pit, can I? And put the charge on my account.'

'Gee, thanks a bunch, Mr . . . erm Vic.'

Lucky's new boss offered him a knowing wink. 'Having you at my back is gonna be worth every penny of that wage I'm paying you.'

* * *

For the next two years, Lucky Johnson made sure that his boss trod a safe path on the streets of Hayes City. He collected the takings from shops owned by Solano and always accompanied him to the bank. Such journeys were now varied on a regular basis.

During that time he dealt with numerous incidents involving unscrupulous tinhorn gamblers, drunken cowpokes and one attempt to rob Solano's house safe.

There was even a threat from a rival

saloon owner called Big Jake Regan who wanted to buy the Dirty Devil at a knockdown price. After being refused, a mysterious fire had broken out in the back store room that nearly burnt the place to the ground.

Lucky discovered Regan sneaking out through the back door. The bodyguard had taken to making a nightly round of Solano's holdings as part of his duties. Now these patrolling stints had paid dividends.

Persuasion to leave Hayes on the next stage was solidly administered by the bodyguard. Along with a bruised body and ego, a proviso was added that if Regan chose to return, his life wouldn't be worth a plugged nickel. The roughneck got the message loud and clear.

Big Jake was never seen again in those parts.

It was during an idle spell when Solano had gone to Denver on business that Lucky found a new way to increase his rapidly growing bank balance even more.

He had been collecting rents from stores owned by the businessman in the nearby settlement of Ellis when he noticed a poster outside the marshal's office. Two hundred bucks was being offered for the apprehension of a half-breed Comanche by the name of Joe Silverheels.

A closer inspection of the details informed him that Silverheels had robbed the Ellis liquor store the previous night and disappeared with his ill-gotten gains. The reward was chickenfeed, but if he could bring this varmint in, perhaps other more lucrative jobs of a similar nature might be forthcoming. He pushed into the law office to make further inquiries.

The marshal was studying a cattle brochure. Brad Stoker was an easygoing sort of guy who preferred to spend his time raising prize Herefords on his smallholding two miles outside town. He reluctantly put the catalogue aside to address his visitor's query.

'That 'breed has been pestering folks

all week for money to spend on fire water,' the town marshal grumbled. 'I was gonna jail the layabout for vagrancy. Then he goes and robs the liquor store of a case of their finest Scotch whisky. Not content with that, he also helped himself to the week's takings. And because he's fled the town limits, I can't go after him.'

Lucky gave the strange comment a puzzled frown.

'Outside my jurisdiction,' remarked Stoker with a regretful shrug. Although Lucky couldn't help noticing the guy seemed almost pleased that the responsibility had been lifted from his shoulders. 'That's why I've posted that reward the owners have put up.'

'Any notion as to where the thief could have headed?' asked Lucky accepting a steaming mug of coffee.

Stoker rubbed his chin in thought.

'My guess is that he'll want to settle down for a blow out with all that tasty liquor. Some place where nobody will find him.' Stoker angled a mindful look at his visitor. 'There ain't many places like that around here. Too darned flat.'

The marshal paused, trying to conjure up a pertinent suggestion. Lucky waited, his patience wearing thin. Then a smile lit up the lawman's dour features. He snapped his fingers.

'Gotta be in the woods by Cedar Bluff Lake.' His bullet head nodded vigorously. 'Ain't no other spot he could hunker down.'

That was all Lucky needed to know.

Cedar Bluff was an isolated hunk of rock stuck in the middle of the plains like an inflamed wart. The so-called excuse for a lake was a reed-choked pond resting in its shadow. A cluster of ponderosa pine enclosed the muddy waters on two sides. It was well off the main trail, which meant that nobody moseyed along that way.

Except on this occasion; a single set of hoof prints pointed directly to the bluff. Lucky shook his head. This guy was greener than a well-tended lawn. He hadn't even bothered to cover his tracks. Nearing the prominent land-mark, the tracker dismounted some quarter mile distant and proceeded the rest of the way on foot.

Circling round to the right, he made his way cautiously through the array of boulders at the foot of the bluff. Ten minutes later, he came upon the object of his quest. A loose smile broke across the craggy features. The Comanche 'breed was splayed on the ground, his boots dabbling in the muddy reach. And spread all around him were empty bottles.

Joe Silverheels was out cold, snoring his head off.

Lucky drew his gun, just in case the 'breed was playing possum.

'On your feet, mister,' he rapped, toeing the recumbent form. 'You're under arrest.' There was no response. A second rather more forceful kick proved just as ineffective.

Lucky smiled to himself. This was like taking candy from a baby. Uncer-emoniously, he heaved the dead weight onto the Indian's own pony and tied him to the saddle.

The trip back to Ellis was uneventful. Only when they reached the town limits did Silverheels come to life. Groans and gurgled imprecations croaked out demanding to know what was happening. Lucky untied the moaning felon and dragged him into the marshal's office. Silverheels reeled and tottered, struggling unsuccessfully to keep his feet.

Stoker's face wrinkled in disgust as the rancid odour of stale alcohol filled the office. The 'breed soon found out what was in store for him when the lawman quickly bundled him out back into the hoosegow.

After returning to the office, Stoker went across to a heavy iron safe in the corner. He extracted a wad of greenbacks and somewhat reluctantly handed them to the novice bounty hunter.

'Here's your dough, mister.' A rather disdainful smirk crossed the leering visage. 'Bet that's the easiest money you ever made.' Lucky couldn't disagree with him. 'Don't spend it all at once,' smirked the lawman.

The scornful retort was lost on the bodyguard who left the office in a buoyant mood. His thoughts were already moving towards the furtherance of a new career.

And so it turned out.

That was the first of numerous other such undertakings. But none proved as easy of attainment as that involving Joe Silverheels.

Over the next couple of years, time passed quickly for Lucky Johnson. Life was good in Hayes City. He had become a man of substance commanding respect.

But like many things in life, the day comes when a guy feels the exigency to move on, seek pastures new, discover what lies over the next hill. But there were other more serious issues bugging the conscientious guardian.

Not least of which was the pressing need to discover his true identity. This had been niggling at the back of his mind for some months. He just needed something to spur him into action.

That moment arrived for Lucky Johnson early one fine Tuesday morning.

He was ambling down the boardwalk for his usual meeting with the boss. Birds twittered overhead, folks bid him good day. On passing the marshal's office, he paused to scan the array of wanted posters and other snippets of information pinned up on the notice board.

The secondary occupation of bounty hunting was beginning to pall. Chasing after wanted felons was dangerous work. His current job didn't pay as much but was infinitely less demanding of time and energy.

Then a languid eye settled on one particular poster. A puzzled frown puckered the high forehead — something was eating at his insides, tugging at his failed memory. He stroked his smooth chin, and looked closer, striving to reach back into the hazy past. Something about that face pricked at his subconscious. It was a roughly drawn depiction but . . .

That was when a fanfare of bugles rang out inside his head. His jaw tightened, body tensing as the penny dropped. Blood drained from his face as two gaping eyes fastened on to the name emblazoned in bold capitals.

Idaho Black! In rapid succession two other names were added to that loathed sobriquet — *Mingus Charlie Brucker* and *Butte Fresno.*

And suddenly the whole sordid episode on Epitaph Ridge at the end of the war shunted into place. Clear as a bell, he could see the events as if they had occurred yesterday. He almost fell down with the shocking revelation. Grimly he clung on to a veranda support.

'You OK, Lucky?' inquired the owner of a perfume store who was passing and had noticed his sudden faintness.

'Y-yeh, m-much obliged, Miss

Charleston,' stammered Lucky shaking off the stunning effect of the eventful occurrence. 'Just a bit light-headed from an over-indulgence of Vic's latest batch of French wine last night.'

'Well you take it easy, young man,' chided the elderly spinster not without a degree of womanly concern.

Lucky Johnson seemed to have that effect on women as a whole. He gave the lady's clement rebuke a contrite nod.

Quickly regaining his composure, Lucky also recalled that his real name was Cody Montaine.

Cody Montaine. He mumbled it out loud. It sounded strange after all this time. Anxiously he peered around. The storekeeper had moved off. Nobody else had noticed the bodyguard's strange reaction. He grabbed hold of the offending poster and tore it off the board. Sitting down on a seat outside the office, he carefully perused the details of the outlaw's offences.

It appeared that Idaho Black must

have split with his other buddies and branched out on his own. Stagecoach robbery and murder had earned the varmint a bounty of one thousand dollars. The money was substantial, but it was immaterial as far as Cody Montaine was concerned. Far more important were the last known whereabouts of the skunk.

So how should he go about handling this sudden shift in fortune?

Remaining in Hayes City was now out of the question. He was going after Black. Only then could he possibly have a chance of catching up with the two other scumbags. But Cody Montaine would have to be kept under wraps. No sense in alerting anybody once he got close to his prey.

Lucky Johnson he would remain. Only when this whole sorry business had been sorted to his satisfaction could he entertain the hope of getting his life back on track.

A fresh gleam of determination twinkled in his eye as he pushed into the marshal's office.

'Howdie there, Lucky,' the ageing lawdog greeted his visitor. 'Come to check on Randy St Clare? He's sleeping it off in the cell out back. That shindig he caused last night is gonna set him back fifty bucks in damages to the saloon plus his fine.'

Lucky ignored the lawman's query. He slapped the wanted poster on the desk. 'You any notion as to where this jigger hangs out, Marshal?' he asked, jabbing a finger at the penned portrait of the villain.

Brad Stoker threw a wary look at the well-dressed bodyguard. His inquiring mind wondered why Vic Solano's right-hand man would suddenly be interested in wanted outlaws.

Up until now, Lucky had kept his pursuit of wanted felons secret. He had no wish to advertise the fact that he doubled as a bounty hunter. It would have jeopardized his standing in Hayes City. Any information he had gleaned was while visiting other towns.

'Any particular reason for inquiring after this fella?' Stoker posed studying the younger man's face for his reaction.

'It's nothing really,' replied Lucky adding a casual shrug of indifference. 'But I seem to recall he was in my regiment during the war.'

The answer appeared to satisfy Stoker.

'Last I heard he'd robbed a stage at Pawnee Rock on the far side of Great Bend. The driver said he was heading southwest.'

'When was that?'

'Two weeks back,' snorted Stoker pouring himself a cup of coffee. 'My reckoning is that he'll be spending his ill-gotten gains in Dodge City right about now.'

At that moment, a muted howl of anguish penetrated the thick walls of the cell block.

'That'll be St Clare coming out of his hangover.' The marshal adjusted his gunbelt and poured a fresh cup of the strong black coffee. 'This'll soon bring the knucklehead back to normality. Anything else you want to know, Lucky?'

The bodyguard shook his head. 'Just a casual interest in an old comrade-in-arms is all. Much obliged.' Then he headed for the door leaving the marshal nursing a nonplussed expression in addition to the hot coffee. But he soon had other things to occupy his thoughts.

'You out there, Marshal?' came the anguished groan from the next room. 'I ain't feelin' too good.'

Stoker raised his eyes skyward. Was he a nursemaid as well as a fount of information? Lucky Johnson's strange inquiry was forgotten. 'Hold on, Randy. I'm a-coming with your coffee.'

4

Old Hostilities

Three miles out of town, Lucky drew his horse to a halt atop a low rise. He looked back towards the cluster of buildings that comprised Hayes City. On three sides, stock pens advertised the town's *raison d'être*. Beyond, in all directions, the rolling grasslands of the prairies reached out to the horizon.

His gaze drifted to the south where a yellow dust-cloud indicated the approach of yet another herd moving slowly up the trail.

Lucky recalled how his own fortunes had changed since that last drive. Now perhaps he could finally draw a line under a dark chapter of his life.

Vic Solano had been sorry to see him go; a bonus had been added to the ex-bodyguard's final wage packet. Once the businessman had been appraised of Lucky's sudden memory recall and its implications, he had wished him luck in his quest.

They had both laughed at the play on words.

'Luck ain't gonna play a part in things when I catch up to those critters,' emphasized the nemesis, the granite expression assuming a more solemn cast. 'Only when them pesky varmints are dead and buried can Lucky Johnson start up afresh as Cody Montaine.'

He tipped his hat to Hayes City, then disappeared over the lip. Would he ever come back this way again? The question was left hanging in the air as he headed southwest across the wind-swept plains of the Kansas prairie.

* * *

It took four days of steady riding to reach Dodge City, yet hours before the growing settlement hove into view,

Lucky could smell it. A rancid odour permeated the air. And the abandoned detritus of slaughtered buffalo testified to its source.

The fort to the east of the town was one of many that were built across the western frontier to control the Indians and protect the growing numbers of settlers heading west for a new life. Originally named Buffalo City for obvious reasons, it was renamed in 1872 after the renowned army colonel who founded the nearby fort.

The rapidly increasing influx all needed feeding. And the massive herds of free-roaming buffalo provided the perfect solution. The pelts were also highly sought after. Even the bones were not wasted.

But it was the plains' tribes that suffered as the buffalo herds were rapidly decimated. Their lifestyle depended on these lumbering goliaths of the plains. With their decline, more and more Indians were forced on to the hated reservations.

By 1872 Dodge was getting into its stride. Within a few years it would become the wildest cow town west of the Mississippi. Lucky's face creased in a wary frown as he recalled a recent newspaper commentator describing Dodge City as the *'beautiful, bibulous Babylon of the trail'*.

With that thought in mind, he nudged his horse slowly into the town's broad main thoroughfare.

Front Street was a chaotic amalgam of single-storey shacks and canvas tents. No boardwalks had yet been added for the convenience of pedestrians. His eye was drawn to the hill behind where the town's cemetery was located. It had acquired the euphemistic name of Boot Hill due to an over-subscription of residents who came to a violent end. Lucky promised himself that he would not be joining them.

A few stock pens on the edge of town indicated that Texas cattle herds were beginning to arrive. The Atchison-Topeka railroad had recently come to

Dodge making for a shorter drive up the trail.

Eagle eyes panned the busy street.

A tense hand rested on the butt of his six-shooter. Even at that very moment, Idaho Black could be weighing up this new stranger in town. There was little chance of the outlaw recognizing his old sergeant. Lucky had grown a thick curling moustache and put on some extra pounds during his time in Hayes. Still, it paid to be cautious.

So where would a guy flush with dough make for in a berg like this?

The obvious answer was the biggest saloon. And that was the Long Branch. Its notoriety had spread east to Hayes City; Lucky was sure that Black would have headed there like a moth to a flame.

He pushed on along the street keeping a watch for the famous bordello.

And there it was, smack in the middle of town. Drawing his lathered horse to a halt, he dismounted and tied up to the hitching rail next to three others. Judging by the tack and brands, they were army mounts. That was to be expected. After all, this was a military base.

Caution weighed heavily as he peered through the grubby window. But there was no sign of his quarry. Various games of chance were being played at the far end of the long narrow room. Gingerly he pushed open the door and stepped inside the gloomy interior. An alcoholic fuzz assailed his senses. Combined with body odour and stale tobacco smoke, this was clearly a place where a man was encouraged to drink hard while gambling away the rest of his poke.

He stepped up to the bar.

'What'll it be, stranger?' inquired the rotund barkeep.

'A cold beer and some information,' came back the blunt reply.

'Beer is fine, but information?' The 'keep shook his head. 'In my experience it's a heap safer to keep a tight lip.

Anything you need to know, ask the town marshal.'

He was about to draw the beer when a five dollar bill was slipped into his shirt pocket.

'Is that enough to ease the tightness?'

'Another of the same could sure help,' smirked the 'keep pushing a foaming glass towards the newcomer. 'Although I can't promise to give the answers you're seeking.'

A second five spot was held just out of reach of the guy's searching hand.

'It's all your'n if you can tell me the whereabouts of a weasel who goes under the handle of Idaho Black.' Lucky held the guy's shifty gaze. 'I'm trying to catch up with him.'

'He a friend of your'n?'

'We're acquainted.' Lucky waggled the note. It was like a tantalizing lure to a hungry trout.

'He was in here. About a week ago. Then he left. Said he'd run out of dough and needed to get a fresh supply.'

'Where did he go?' Lucky sipped his beer, the steady eye pinning the bartender to the spot.

The beerpuller stroked his fleshy chin thoughtfully. 'Now where was it he said he was going? Urm! Can't quite recall,' he huffed trying to give the impression that another hand-out might stimulate his memory.

Lucky's face was set in stone. Then his left hand shot out and grabbed the simpering toad by the throat.

'Now listen up good, you overblown tub of lard.' Little more than a whisper, the curt rasp hissed like steam from a boiling kettle. 'Ten bucks is all you're gonna get. Now spill the beans or taste your own blood.' A small switchblade tickling the guy's thick neck encouraged an honest reply.

'Y-yes, s-sir,' quaked the sweating barman. 'H-he was bound f-for Amarillo. It's in the Texas — '

'I know where it is, dummy,' the gruff retort interjected, adding, 'You sure of that?' The knife dug a little deeper.

'S-sure I am. He was b-bragging about a dame down that way he was gonna have his way with when he came into some serious money.'

Lucky sucked in a lungful of air, then released the gut bucket.

A five dollar bonus fluttered down on to the bar top. It was immediately swept up by a pudgy hand as the 'keep hustled away to regain his composure.

Lucky wasted no more time in the Long Branch. There was still enough daylight for another couple of hours' riding. He downed the rest of his beer then exited the saloon.

But he was not alone.

Three army privates slouching at the end of the bar had witnessed the fracas with the bartender, but that wasn't of any concern to the the Fort Dodge troopers. It was what the stranger was wearing that had caught their interest. In particular, his hat. Even beneath the layer of trail dust, the grey of the Confederate Army with its crossed swords badge was clearly identifiable.

Some years had passed since the end of the war. Yet still a degree of antagonism existed between the opposing factions. Most of the time it remained dormant, but sometimes, a reminder of the suffering endured caused old hatreds to resurface.

And these guys had already consumed a serious quantity of hard liquor. They were ready for some action. And Lucky Johnson would provide it.

The object of their aggression was checking the leathers of his saddle when the challenge rang out.

'Hey, Reb!' The defiance was blunt and forthright. It was the insulting appellation that all southerners hated. 'Low-life scum that support slavery ain't welcome in Dodge. Truth is, your kind ain't welcome anyplace where decent folks live.'

The speaker was a burly hatchet-faced dude. He was accompanied by two equally tough-looking critters. All were dressed in cavalry blues, their hands resting on holstered Army

Remington pistols.

'Now you take off that hat and stamp it into the dust,' rasped the leader of the trio. 'Then we'll know that you're ashamed to be associated with them cottonpickin' johnnies. You hear me, Reb?'

Lucky eyed the three men. He had come across this sort before and found it best to ignore the threats. Most of the time a few shouted insults were all that followed, although occasionally, more direct action was needed.

These guys looked as if they were not about to be ignored. All the same, he swung up into the saddle and prepared to move off.

'This varmint needs teaching a lesson,' growled one of the men stepping forward to grab a hold of the reins.

'Let go if'n you value your mangy hide.' The threat was laced with smoldering menace as Lucky dragged his horse away from the reaching paws.

'Get him, boys!' yelled the leader of the bunch.

All three went for their guns.

Lucky immediately swung low across the far side of his mount. Gripping the horse's withers, he leant under its neck while palming his own shooter. Guns blasted but the soldier boys' target had disappeared. Bullets whistled by harmlessly overhead burying themselves in the wooden buildings on the far side of the street.

Now it was the turn of the rider.

Two shots burned the air. One of the soldiers staggered back, struck in the chest. He was dead before his body hit the ground. Another spun on his boot heels, caught in the shoulder.

Lucky rolled out of the saddle on to the ground and hunkered behind a nearby water trough. After judging the fire to have been well and truly quenched, he slowly hauled himself to his feet. His gun swung to cover the third man.

'Your play, mister,' he said calmly aiming the pistol at the remaining trooper who was unscathed. 'See to your injured buddy or join the other bastard in hell.'

The stunned private ogled his two associates. But he still had the good sense to keep his hands well clear of his hardware. Then he backed off.

'OK, mister, don't shoot,' he pleaded helping his moaning Confederate to his feet. 'It was Fagan's doin'. That big mouth of his soundin' off agin. Now he's paid the price.' Heaving his wounded partner off the ground, the sorry pair moved off up the street in the direction of the town sawbones.

Lucky's gun hand remained steady as he remounted his horse. His piercing gaze followed the recent troublemakers, just in case.

A whiskey-soured voice close by broke his concentration.

'Take my advice, fella,' counselled an old buffalo skinner who had witnessed the entire ruction. 'Hit the trail and don't look back. The army don't take kindly to its men gettin' shot up. Them dudes stick together. They don't give a damn who started the hoohah.'

Lucky nodded his thanks to the old timer.

'Much obliged,' he said. 'I'll keep that in mind.'

'Where you headed, son?' inquired the old timer.

'Got me some business that needs sorting in Amarillo,' replied the pensive rider, his eyes narrowing to thin slits as the odious features of Idaho Black swam into his vision.

The sombre cast was not lost on the perceptive skinner.

'Then you take care, y'hear? There's some mighty bad dudes down that way.'

A half-smile cracked the stoic demeanour. Lucky dug into his pocket and extracted a dollar piece. Flicking it into the air, he remarked. 'That's sound advice, mister. Have a drink on Lucky Johnson. And while you're at it, raise a toast to me catching up with a lowdown snake called Idaho Black.'

The skinner's eyes widened as he caught the glinting disc. The inevitable tooth test as to its authenticity followed.

'You sure have set yourself a risky task, young fella,' clucked the old guy shaking his head. 'That's the varmint who shot the marshal only last week. The price on his head will surely have doubled. Not to mention the danger to anyone hopin' to claim it.'

★   ★   ★

Three days later, a faded sign informed the dusty rider that he was leaving Kansas. Underneath, a facetious wit had scrawled in red — *Welcome to No Man's Land!*

Lucky's jaw tightened as he recalled the warning of the old buffalo skinner. He was now entering a narrow strip of abandoned wasteland between Texas, Indian Territory and Kansas, where nobody held jurisdiction. As such it had become a retreat for all manner of brigands. With no law enforcement agency willing to take responsibility for the policing of the panhandle, it was an outlaw's paradise.

The notion occurred to Lucky that Idaho Black might well have decided to take up residence here. But the bartender of the Long Branch in Dodge had been emphatic that Amarillo was his destination.

So that town remained the hunter's also.

5

Eye For An Eye

'The lady's waitin' on your answer, fella,' pressed Kirk Diamond. 'Just like the rest of us.'

The cutting remark jerked Lucky out of his musing reverie. He shook the cobwebs free. Four pairs of curious peepers fastened on to him.

'Guess the tinhorn is right at that,' Lucky shot back, injecting the gambler's biting insinuation with his own brand of waspish delivery.

Diamond scowled, but let the threatening undertone pass. His time would come. He shifted his surly gaze back to the solo card game.

Lucky reached into his pocket and removed a crumpled sheet of paper which he placed on his knee.

'This is the guy I'm after,' he said

softly, a lump forming in his throat. 'Some guys are just felons that need their wings clipping. Money in the bank. With this varmint' — he swallowed as the recall surged to the fore — 'it's personal.'

The distant glassy-eyed cast returned for a brief moment to be replaced by a hard glint.

'Mind if I see that?' asked Mason.

Lucky passed the sheet to the cowpoke who proceeded to read out the particulars of the wanted owlhoot's crimes. It was fortunate for Kirk Diamond that the other passengers were concentrating on Cal Mason's utterance. Consequently, nobody noticed the ashen look that had invaded the gambler's pasty features.

That was the moment a warning holler from the stagecoach driver interrupted Mason's outflow.

'There's four jaspers up ahead that are actin' mighty suspicious,' Crackajack Muldoon called down. 'They look like road agents to me. You folks keep your heads down while I whip up the horses. Ain't no way I'm gettin' robbed again. This'll be the second time in a month.'

A sharp whipsnap cut through the fetid atmosphere. It was immediately followed by a full-blown whoop of determination from the stubborn driver as the pace of the coach suddenly picked up. They were all forced to grab a hold of the loops attached to the roof provided for the express purpose of traversing rough terrain.

Mason ignored the driver's advice by sticking his head out the window. His mouth opened wide on catching sight of the riders up ahead. Ducking back inside, he quickly scanned the wanted dodger. 'Looks like you'll be meeting up with this dude sooner 'n you thought, mister.' He pointed to one of the riders. 'Take a look see!'

Lucky's narrowed gaze followed the cowpoke's jabbing arm. His eyes widened in shock. The kid was right: it was Idaho Black himself. And the skunk had assembled a gang.

Just then, the relative quiet inside the bucking coach was punctuated by a sharp report. Heads swivelled towards its source as smoke filled the confined space. Kirk Diamond's left hand was clutching at a rapidly spreading blood-stain on his chest. A small .32 Slocum pocket pistol slipped from nerveless fingers on to the floor of the coach along with his valise.

Miss Harper screamed, a fearful hand covering her mouth.

But it was towards the other occupant of the coach that eyes now swivelled.

The preacher was clutching a small Remington double derringer. Smoke dribbled from one of the twin barrels. Exhibiting a deft flourish, the reverend gent crossed himself before replacing the pistol in the inside pocket of his black suit.

'The good Lord helps those who help themselves,' opined the preacher in a suitably dolorous voice. He offered a solemn bow to the bleeding corpse.

'And Mr Diamond here was about to do the dirty on you two boys. So it was incumbent upon me as a servant of God to even up the situation by neutralizing an underhanded critter engaged in the Devil's work.'

A pair of hooded eyes lifted in a suitably grave acknowledgement to his Boss. Then, without any compunction, he opened the coach door on the far side, grabbed a hold of the lifeless body and flung it unceremoniously outside.

It was a bizarre and decidedly uncharacteristic act from a preacher, but one for which the remaining passengers were more than grateful. No time was available for further speculation: the robbers now required their urgent attention.

'He must have been in cahoots with the gang out there,' exclaimed Mason, drawing his own revolver. 'The treacherous snake was hoping to make it easier for them to rob us.'

Gunfire broke out up ahead indicating that the driver's suspicions had been well founded. The whip cracked again as the die-hard driver urged the team of six to their limits.

'Come on, me beauties,' yelled Muldoon defiantly. 'Let's show these low-lifes what we're made of.' The six horses responded with vigour. Ears flattened, legs straining, they surged forward.

Lucky pushed the girl roughly to the floor. This was no time for pussyfooting about.

'Do what the driver says, gal, and keep your head down,' he rapped firmly. Miss Harper voiced no objection to the brusque treatment. 'There's gonna be a heap of lead flying soon.'

Then he tossed his revolver to the preacher. 'Seeing as how the good Lord has seen fit to give you some earthly defence against vermin, use this on that side of the coach. It'll do a sight more damage than that peashooter.'

Farrow sniffed. 'It sure got rid of the Judas in our midst, didn't it?' he reciprocated with potency.

'And for that we'll be eternally in your debt,' concurred Lucky, not wishing to denigrate the preacher's vital input. 'But a six-shooter has more firepower and range.'

Without waiting for a response he levered a round into the barrel of his Henry carbine and leaned out the window. Clouds of dust blurred the images of the attacking bandits. Three shots rang out as Lucky aimed for the nearest assailant. He had the pleasure of hearing a yelp of pain as the jasper disappeared from view.

Mason uttered a whoop of triumph as he avidly joined in.

But all did not go their way. A groan from the driver's bench informed the passengers that Muldoon had been hit. Someone would have to climb out and take charge of the horses otherwise the whole caboodle would likely crash. A wheel hitting a stray rock would be calamitous.

Lucky handed his rifle to the young cowhand.

'Keep 'em busy while I take over up top,' he yelled above the crackle of gunfire. It was not the first time he had been in this bleak situation.

Back in '67, Lucky had taken a job riding shotgun for the Remington Arms Company. A band of marauding Delaware Indians had tried unsuccessfully to upgrade their ancient stock of weaponry by attacking one of the convoys.

The driver of Lucky's wagon had been killed. The shotgun guard had taken over the reins until such time as the renegades had been beaten off. A second wagon had not been as fortunate. It had been smashed to pieces after striking a rock.

Mason needed no second bidding. He blasted away as Lucky squirmed through the narrow window. The wind caught his hat, which whirled away into the murk. Grabbing a hold of the upper luggage rail, he scrambled out on to the roof and slid down beside the wounded driver.

'You able to hold on, Crackajack?' shouted Lucky taking hold of the flapping leathers. The long bull-whip had disappeared.

The old driver replied with a weak nod. He was bleeding from a shoulder wound. 'A pesky scratch like this ain't gonna stop me,' he rasped even though it was clear that the bullet had done considerable damage.

'Then hold on tight!' hollered the new driver, ''cos we ain't stopping for nobody, least of all a bunch of thieving road agents.'

Another bandit threw up his arms and tumbled from the saddle.

'Yeehaah!' came the caustic retort from below. 'That's done for another of the skunks.'

The rich baritone cadence had only one source. Clearly the Reverend Amos Farrow had decided to fully commit himself to the onerous task into which he had become unwittingly embroiled; the adrenalin was flowing thick and fast in the preacher's veins.

He did, however, remember to temper the outburst with a suitable Bible quotation to justify the terminal action.

'And as the good books says, an eye for an eye.'

'Can't argue with that,' grinned Lucky.

Faced with all this unexpected opposition to his planned robbery, Idaho Black decided to cut his losses and call it a day. Three of his men were down including their ace in the hole, Kirk Diamond. Only Fireball Tom Jaggs was left unscathed.

The guy had acquired his odd nickname after torching the Sundance Saloon in Witchita when the owner had claimed he was cheating at cards. Jaggs had vehmently denied the assertion. That night he had poured coal oil over the tinder dry walls and set them alight. As a result, much of the town had gone up in flames.

Jaggs had thoroughly enjoyed the sight from atop a knoll outside the town.

'Let's scarper!' Black yelled above the raucous din. 'Things are gettin' a sight too hot around here.'

Fireball Jaggs needed no second bidding. He swung his mount away and followed Black.

The passengers all erupted in a bout of strident cheering. Even Crackajack Muldoon joined in the festivities. Once he was sure that the varmints were not hiding up ahead, Lucky brought the team to a dignified halt. A family of gophers popped up on the far side of the trail to see what all the rumpus was about. Close by, a jackrabbit pelted for the cover of some boulders.

'Better get you inside, fella,' remarked the vigilant relief driver.

Muldoon nodded. 'There's a medical box in the trunk. Maybe one of these good folks can render some first aid until we reach Cimarron.'

'I'll attend to Mr Muldoon.' Felicity Harper had quickly tidied herself up following the rather undignified placement on the coach floor. 'I have done some nursing at the hospital in St Louis.'

Once Crackajack was settled inside the coach, Lucky clambered back up on to the front seat, and urged the team of six back into motion. This time the pace was more sedate. Not only for the comfort of the wounded driver, but Lucky wanted to keep a circumspect eye open for any further chicanery from the wily Idaho Black.

He needn't have worried.

* * *

The outlaw and his accomplice were camped out in a draw well off the main trail where they were licking their wounds. This had been Black's third foray on the owlhooter trail. The previous two heists had gone according to plan with Kirk Diamond playing his part to perfection.

Something had clearly gone wrong. He could not have foreseen that a maverick preacher had been the cause of the fiasco.

The two outlaws were hunched around a small fire sipping hot coffee. A rabbit was sizzling on a spit.

'Can't figure out what went wrong,' grumbled Jaggs morosely.

Black stared into the fire. 'Diamond must have been sussed,' he submitted, irritation edging the blunt riposte. 'The durned fool must have pulled his gun too soon and been spotted.'

Jaggs lifted the rabbit off the spit and sawed a leg off, which he proceeded to chew on. 'At least I nailed that ole coot drivin' the coach,' he spluttered spitting out a mouthful of gristle.

'But they shot up two of the boys,' retorted Black grimacing at the stringy hunk of rabbit, 'and we end up stuck out here, still broke when we should be in the dough.'

'So what we gonna do?' voiced his partner tossing away the picked bone.

Black's skeletal visage creased in thought. After a long minute he made a decision. After all, that's why he was the leader of this two-bit outfit.

'I reckon we should head north to Las Vegas,' pondered Black lighting up a cheroot. 'Got me a buddy up there who'll give us a job.'

'Hear tell that's one wide open berg,' remarked Jaggs, adding a generous measure of whiskey to his coffee. 'Do I know this jasper?' he inquired.

'Fella by the name of Fresno,' replied Black. 'We were in the same unit during the war.' He scoffed as the memories of that last day flooded back. 'Got out just in time otherwise we'd have been pushin' up the daisies with all the other suckers on Epitaph Ridge.'

Jaggs considered the name thoughtfully.

'That ain't Butte Fresno, is it?'

Black arrowed his sidekick with a questioning frown. 'You two acquainted?'

Jaggs laughed. 'He's the critter that gave me the moniker of Fireball after we had to hightail it from Witchita.'

Black joined in with the hilarity. 'Well

I'll be a goldarned son of a sidewinder,'
he hollered. 'Now don't that beat all.'

'Maybe things are lookin' up after
all,' Jaggs guffawed sniffing the appreciative aroma of a Havana cigar.

6

Mixed Fortunes

It took a half day of steady jogging for the stagecoach to reach Cimarron. Lucky drew the team to a halt outside the Butterfield office. A small bald-headed dude hustled out to meet the arrival. His mouth dropped open on seeing a stranger riding up front.

'Where's Crackajack?' he snapped acidly. Bullet holes in the woodwork did not augur well.

Lucky stepped down before replying. Ignoring the flustered official, he helped Miss Harper out of the coach. Only then did he deign to address the hovering clerk.

'We were attacked by a gang of bushwackers — '

'Did they get the strong box?' butted in the sweating agent, whose sole concern was for the stage's cargo.

Lucky's response to the obdurate inquiry was an ascerbic glower.

'No, they didn't!' he rasped. 'But they did shoot your driver before we managed to scare them off.' Lucky stuck his stony visage to within an inch of the little guy's twitching snout. 'Glad to see the Butterfield stage company is so concerned for its employees.' The heavy dose of sarcasm was not lost on the simpering clerk, whose round face turned redder than the setting sun. 'Now maybe you could organize a sawbones for this poor guy.'

The Reverend Farrow and Cal Mason were helping the injured Crackajack Muldoon out of the coach.

The clerk gasped on seeing the blood-smeared effigy.

'Y-yes, s-sir, immediately, sir,' he burbled.

A crowd of bystanders had gathered to witness the unusual event. Even in a town like Cimarron, it wasn't every day that a stagecoach was attacked.

'Hyram!' hollered the clerk. 'Come out here straight away.'

An underling scurried out of the office. 'What is it, Mr Niblick?' he asked innocently.

'Go and get Doc Turner to come here right away.'

The young assistant ambled away.

'Run, you lazy faggot!' balled Agent Niblick, trying to regain some degree of authority.

The virulent kickass did the trick. Ribald comments followed the coaching assistant's hurried progress down the main street, much to Tucker Niblick's satisfaction.

With the preacher and cowboy attending to the injured driver, Lucky was able to devote himself to Miss Harper. Taking her by the arm, he led the willing woman across the street towards what appeared to be the most salubrious hotel in Cimarron.

The Regal Crown was able to book the young lady into a suitable room for the night. Fifteen minutes later, having established herself, Felicity Harper tripped down the ornate staircase. Lucky immediately lumbered to his feet.

'I take it you will be continuing onward in the morning?' he said when she joined him.

There was a distinct lack of enthusiasm in the inquiry. Much to his surprise, Lucky had found himself drawn to the bewitching creature. The fact that she was engaged to another man seemed to have skipped his memory. Most of the women he had encountered on a more personal level since leaving the army were mostly of three kinds: ageing spinsters, wholesomely plain rancher's wives or saloon gals.

This girl was a new experience. One that he would have most assuredly wished to expand upon.

'The stage leaves at eight o'clock sharp.' Her eyes were bright and sparkling with zeal. 'And Mr Salmon, the hotel proprietor, assures me that we will be in Las Vegas within three days.'

Lucky's face assumed a stoically neutral mien. He nodded vaguely, holding out a limp hand. 'Then I hope you will find true happiness,' he intoned with a sombre gravity that went over the girl's head. A lump formed in his throat. 'Seeing as how we might not meet again.'

This closing remark finally got the girl's full attention. She peered at the tall manhunter, and squeezed his hand. A tingle raced down Lucky Johnson's spine. He felt like he was drowning in the girl's limpid gaze.

'I feel certain that we will meet again, Mr Johnson,' she averred firmly. 'And if you pass through Las Vegas, my fiancé and I will be more than happy to see you.'

Lucky forced a smile, although he was less keen on the confirmation that another man came first in Miss Harper's thoughts. Doleful eyes followed as she turned away, sashaying across to the reception desk, there to make inquiries regarding her imminent departure from Cimarron.

The downcast bounty hunter accorded the girl one last lingering sigh, then departed himself to report the attempted robbery to the sheriff. The lawman was able to confirm that Idaho Black's reward had indeed leapt by another five hundred bucks. And Fireball Jaggs had now been added to the wanted list of felons. At least something good might come out of this situation.

Walking back along the street, he met up with Cal Mason. Both men continued down to the livery stable at the end of the street where they had left their horses. The stagecoach was still outside the Butterfield office.

'Looks like the stage is stuck here until they can get a new driver,' observed the cowhand.

Lucky nodded absently. Other more important matters were on his mind.

'What you gonna do now?' asked the eager cowpoke. 'Is that wanted critter still on your agenda?'

'Sure is,' concurred the bounty hunter, 'I'm heading back to where the ambush took place. Should be able to pick up his trail from there. And hopefully the hat I lost.'

Mason shuffled his feet. Lucky sensed that the kid was itching to say something else. He angled a quizzical half-smile towards the young puncher.

'Some'n on your mind, Cal?'

The kid hesitated, not quite knowing how to voice his request.

'Don't suppose you could do with some help, could you?' came back the halting query. Without waiting for an answer, he hurried on spluttering out a torrent of reasons why he should be included in the manhunt. 'I'm good with a gun. Didn't I knock out one of them varmints from a lurching coach? And I don't want a share of the reward. You can keep the whole darned lot far as I'm concerned. I just wanna see this business through to the end.'

If truth be told, Cal Mason was getting bored with the mundane chores imposed by his father on the ranch. This episode with the bandits had only served to fuel his yearning for excitement. The youngster fastened a solicitous eye on to the older man, silently urging him towards a positive decision.

Lucky smiled to himself; there was no doubting the kid had guts. And two desperate outlaws on the run would be a dangerous undertaking to accomplish alone. Still, he maintained a flat expression. The kid was on tenterhooks.

'Guess I could use an extra gun,' he said eventually. Lucky's gaze hardened as he added with sombre intent, 'Just be aware that going after two hard-boiled gunslingers is no Sunday picnic.' He jabbed a warning finger at the eager young cowpoke. 'And you take orders from me. Savvy?'

'Sure thing, pard, you're the boss,' gushed the ardent kid. 'You got my solemn word on that.'

After collecting their fed and watered mounts, the two riders headed back up

Cimarron's main drag. On the far side, Felicity Harper was making her way down to the stage office to see when the next coach was leaving for Las Vegas. Had the lady known that she would be stuck in Cimarron for another week, she would not have been so upbeat.

Lucky's heart leapt inside his chest. He tipped his hat, a warm smile matching the amatory gleam in his eye. The lady's response was rather less captivating, cool even. A brief lift of the hand, the token acknowledgement, before she disappeared into the office.

Lucky stifled his disappointment by digging spurs into the grey and galloped off in a cloud of dust.

★ ★ ★

It took them the better part of the day to backtrack to where the stagecoach had been waylaid. The much-valued hat lay where it had fallen in the dust.

Thereafter, a measured pace was essential so as not to miss any chance of spotting where the bandits had left the main trail. Dusk was closing in fast before a shout from Cal Mason heralded the sign for which he had been searching.

'It has to be them,' concurred Lucky verifying the kid's discovery. Bending down, he fingered the dual set of hoof prints. 'Well done, pard. I'd have missed them for sure without your eagle eye.' The praise brought a beaming smile to the cowpoke's face. 'Too late to follow now. We'll set up camp down this draw and head off at first light.'

Morning dawned fine and colourful. Fiery streaks of pink, purple and orange scored the eastern sky as the two hunters sipped their morning brew of Arbuckles. The strong coffee quickly cleared away the cobwebs. Breakfast was two sticks of beef jerky apiece and some biscuits. After packing away their gear, the morning light had strengthend sufficiently to make the trail easy to follow.

The bandits had made no attempt to

conceal their route. Frustration and despondency with the failed robbery had clearly stupefied Idaho Black's shifty brain. Straight as an arrow, the trail pointed southwest across the barren wilderness of the Conchas Sink.

A bleak expanse of undulating flatlands lay before them. Greasewood and catclaw vied for position with the dominant sagebrush and mesquite. Surging clumps of yucca poked above the rim trying to assert their importance with a scattering of creamy white daubs.

'Let's hope we can catch up with the critters afore they disappear into the Turkeys,' observed the anxious hunter pointing to the distant range of corrugated mountains. 'With this trail, they couldn't have done us a bigger favour had they left a map.' His craggy features clouded over. 'But that'll end once they strike the high country.'

He spurred off at a steady lick followed by his eager sidekick.

It was around the noon hour on the

following day that Lucky espied a blue-grey coil of smoke snaking above a cluster of cottonwoods into the shimmering firmament. The landscape was rapidly changing. Foothill terrain below the Turkey range substantially reduced visibility over a distance forcing the pursuers down to a walk.

'That has to be them,' announced Lucky. 'The knuckleheads sure aren't expecting company with a blaze like that.'

'Then they're in for a big surprise,' breezed his buddy eagerly.

Lucky drew his mount to a halt.

'From here we go on foot,' he declared, dismounting. 'You circle round to the left. Then we can catch 'em in a pincer movement.' His old army training had clicked in. Before moving forward, he checked his guns were fully loaded.

Meanwhile, the outlaws were preparing to strike camp.

'I reckon we need to get us some fresh horses at the next ranch we happen on,' remarked an anxious

Fireball Jaggs. 'These nags are plum tuckered out. If it comes to a chase, we ain't got a hope in hell of escapin'.'

Black scoffed at his partner's reticence.

'You worry too much,' he said. 'Nobody's gonna pick up our trail.'

'Maybe I am a bit edgy,' admitted Jaggs. 'Anybody would be after that fiasco with the Santa Fe stage.' Then his voice hardened. 'It should have been better organized.'

'That weren't my fault,' snapped Black angrily as he saddled his horse. 'If Diamond had done his job properly, everything would have gone to plan.'

Jaggs shrugged. 'I'll go rinse the plates and fill up the water bottles from the creek.' He moved off through the trees.

Crouched down low beside the gently swirling watercourse, Jaggs was hidden from view by a clutch of dwarf willows. In consequence, the approaching figure of Lucky Johnson failed to spot him. The hunter was taking extra care to conceal his presence. Nonetheless, a broken twig gave him away.

Jaggs peered through the dense foliage.

'Hell's teeth!' he muttered to himself. So much for Black's confident assertion that nobody would pick up their trail. Quietly, he stood up and drew his pistol. Silent as a shadow, he slunk after the furtive tracker, dogging his every move.

Lucky paused behind a tree near the clearing where the outlaws had made camp. The fact that only one outlaw was there didn't raise any warning signals. They could have split up after fleeing the abortive raid on the stage. He was just about to challenge the unsuspecting Idaho Black when a gruff voice brought Lucky to an abrupt halt.

'Hold it right there, mister.'

Lucky stiffened. When he made to swing round, a warning growl edged with threatening menace terminated the foolhardy move.

'Keep your back to me and drop that

iron!' Cursing to himself for being hoodwinked, Lucky had no choice but to obey the brusque command. 'Now unbuckle that fancy rig and step into the open. Any tricks and there's a .44 hunk of lead coming your way.'

On seeing the stranger emerging from the tree cover, Black leapt to his feet and palmed his own six-gun.

'I spotted this crafty dude sneaking up on the camp,' rasped Jaggs pushing the prisoner forward. 'Seems like he was fixing to pay us an unexpected visit. And packing a fistful of iron ain't the friendliest calling card.'

Eight years had passed since the end of the war. Much had happened in the interim. Lucky Johnson had changed. He had lost a lot of weight and grown a thick moustache. The lustrous mop of black hair had turned prematurely grey adding a sight more than eight years to his age. Living up to his nickname, Lucky was thankful that the skunk did not recognize his old sergeant.

And he had no intention of voicing a reminder.

Idaho Black, however, was still the same weasel-faced varmint he remembered. There was no mistaking those shifty eyes, and the cruel knife-slash of a mouth.

'What's your game, mister?' rapped Black prodding his gun at the prisoner. 'Sneakin' around tryin' to get the drop on us.'

'Got myself lost in the brush.' Lucky raised his voice hoping that his partner would hear and realize that the tables had unfortunately been turned. 'Sorry for creeping about in the trees. But a fella can't be too careful these days with all these bandits about.'

Black spat out a lurid epithet. 'That's a durned lie. My bet is you're after grabbin' the reward for the infamous Idaho Black.' The outlaw proudly jabbed a thumb at his chest, an ugly grin creasing the waxy features. 'Too bad you'll never collect.'

Lucky's blood ran cold as the

owlhoot's gun rose. Outwardly, he showed no sign of fear, but inside his guts turned to jelly. Where was Mason?

Black took his time, enjoying the moment as he racked the hammer to full cock. His sidekick was more impatient. 'Come on, Idaho, get it over with! We ain't got all day.'

That slight delay saved Lucky's life. A scuffling on the far side of the clearing saw the two hardcases whirling to face this unexpected threat.

'Drop your guns,' came the welcome snap from Cal Mason. 'I've got you both covered.'

But Black was not so easily cowed. Without thought, he brought his six-gun round and loosed off two shots. The first struck Cal in the shoulder. The cowboy went down, blood pouring from the bullet hole. Jaggs brought his own gun to bear against Lucky.

As soon as the shooting began, the bounty hunter dropped to the ground. He rolled across to where his own gunbelt had fallen. Bullets from Jaggs's pistol gouged the ground inches from his head.

His own gun roared before Jaggs had a chance to get off a third shot. Orange flame burst from the Remington. Lucky by name, lucky by nature. The nickname paid dividends as the outlaw bit the dust.

'Aaaaagh!'

Jaggs staggered back clutching at the fatal wound in his chest. He crashed into Black who was thrown off balance.

Another shot echoed around the clearing as Lucky attempted to finish off the remaining outlaw. But Jaggs' dead body provided a barricade for the antagonist. Black took full advantage of this unexpected yet providential development. His own gun fired again. Lucky's hat was lifted from his head, the bullet scoring a thin line across his scalp.

It was not a serious injury, but the seering pain was sufficient to deflect his aim. Seeing his chance to escape, Black lurched to his feet and dashed into the nearby undergrowth.

Seeing his quarry disappear, Lucky stumbled to his feet and sought to give chase. But the injury slowed him up allowing the dense foliage to effectively swallow up the fleeing outlaw.

Lucky cursed aloud knowing that his adversary had once again escaped justice. Despondently, he returned to the clearing. Before attending to his partner's wounded shoulder, Lucky checked up on Fireball Jaggs. One glance was enough to inform him that the outlaw had cashed in his chips.

Cal emitted a pained groan on the far side of the clearing as he tried to stem the flow of blood from his wound. It was serious but not life threatening. After cleaning the wound, Lucky tore up one of his spare shirts and bandaged the shoulder.

'You'll be OK until we get back to Cimarron,' announced Lucky. The jaded tone betrayed a sombre melancholy that pervaded his whole being.

Cal instantly picked up on the

downcast mood.

'It was all my fault that Black got away,' he said in a regretful woebegone spirit. 'If I hadn't shilly-shallied, neither of us would have been shot and Black wouldn't have scarpered.'

'Don't blame yourself,' Lucky mollified the doleful cowboy. 'Those varmints were hard-bitten gunslingers, you are a ranch-hand. Anyone faced with killing a man would have hesitated.' Lucky held up his hands. 'I should have been more careful and not allowed them to get the drop on me.'

'At least we got one of the skunks,' Cal brightened as Lucky strapped the cadaver of Fireball Jaggs to the dead outlaw's cayoose.

Soon after, the two hunters left the glade heading back towards Cimarron.

The encounter with Idaho Black, although having an unsuccessful outcome, had triggered the notion that something was still missing from his memory loss. Try as he might, however, Lucky just could not dredge it up from the depths of his being.

There appeared to be a connection with Las Vegas. The town kept nudging at his brain cells. And not just because the lovely Felicity Harper was heading there. Once he'd seen Cal Mason safely back to his father's ranch, a trip to Las Vegas might help fill in that unaccountable gap.

7

A Disturbing Episode

Lucky offered his buddy a half share of the reward money for Fireball Jaggs. But the young cowpoke had been reluctant to accept.

'When it came to the crunch, I flunked out,' he complained morosely. 'Man-to-man, I just didn't have what it takes. Guess I ain't a hard-boiled rannie after all. Just an ordinary cowpoke who's only good enough for shooting rabbits and rattlers.'

Lucky fastened a probing eye on the youngster. 'If'n you hadn't drawn their attention when you did, I'd have been crowbait. Black was all set to gun me down.'

He pushed the wad of greenbacks into the kid's hand. 'Take it!' he insisted. 'I won't take no for an answer.

Maybe the experience will persuade you that cowpunching ain't so bad after all. It's a noble profession and a heap safer than going after gun-happy owlhoots.'

Cal reluctantly accepted. The gnawing ache in his recently dressed shoulder was enough to convey the notion that Lucky was right. He would stick with what he knew best and leave gunslinging to tough guys like Lucky Johnson.

They headed south from Cimarron with the soaring wall of the Sangre de Cristo Mountains on their right. The terrain this side of the foothills offered excellent grazing for prime beef cattle.

Meadowlarks and jays swooped and frolicked amidst the stands of Douglas fir and ponderosa pine. A pair of chipmunks capered playfully nearby.

'This is good country, Cal,' noted Lucky admiring the scenery. 'A guy would be foolish to opt for anything different.'

Having tasted life on the other side of

the trail, Cal wholeheartedly concurred. Two days of steady riding saw the cowboy pointing out the first longhorns sporting his home Box Bar M brand.

They reached the extended log cabin and outbuildings of the ranch around late afternoon. Rough-hewn, the Box Bar M was one of numerous small spreads that had taken advantage of the rich grazing afforded by the waters of the Gallinas River. A tributary of the mighty Pecos, it watered the rolling grassland that enabled cattle to fatten up ready for the drive to market.

A man was standing in the doorway of the main house.

Tall and well built with iron-grey hair, he held a Loomis shotgun loosely across his broad chest. Howard Mason was taking no chances. These were difficult times for ranchers in the Gallinas valley.

Only two weeks previously, Joe Carter of the Zed Bend had been forced to sell up for a knockdown price after his place had mysteriously gone up in smoke. It was a strange coincidence that the so-called accident had occurred only a week after he had refused to sell up when a stranger had called by.

So far no approach had been made to buy the Box Bar M. But Mason was under no illusions that he would not be targeted.

The heavily ribbed forehead softened when Mason saw the white arm sling supporting his son's injured shoulder. He put down the gun and hurried over to greet the two riders.

'What happened to you?' he shot out anxiously peering from his son to the stranger accompanying him.

'It ain't nothing, Pa,' replied Cal trying to play down the seriousness of his injury. 'Me and Lucky here ran into some outlaws who tried to rob the Santa Fe stage.' The youngster tried to square his shoulders but the effort brought a pained gasp. He forced a smile. 'We managed to chase 'em off.'

'Tell me about it later,' the rancher butted in helping his son to dismount.

'Maybe first you should introduce me to your friend.' He eyed the stranger with a blank, somewhat suspicious frown. All newcomers to the ranch these days were regarded with distrust, until their veracity was proven.

'Meet Lucky Johnson, Pa,' said Cal, pride showing in his beaming face. 'He's a — '

Lucky jumped in before the impetuous boy could reveal his true profession.

'I'm a concerned citizen who don't take kindly to being shot at by road agents. We went after the gang but one of them got away. Your son helped to' — he paused, searching for the right words — 'to deal with the other one. He's been a dependable partner and I'm more'n grateful that he saved my life. You should be proud of him.'

'And I earned myself a wad of dough too,' exhorted Cal. 'Fireball Jaggs had a price on his head.'

Mason did not share his son's euphoria. The tooled leather gun rig with its cross-over holster told him all he needed to know. Hooded eyes and a tight-lipped regard indicated his disapproval. He turned to address the tall stranger knowing exactly the sort of guy he was facing.

'I don't take kindly to gunfighters encouraging my kin to join in their dangerous manhunting activities,' he murmured holding the other man's stoical gaze with an equally hard glint.

'Don't blame Lucky, Pa,' urged Cal. 'I persuaded him to let me tag along. But I've learned my lesson the hard way. I ain't no gunhawk that's for sure. From here on, I'm sticking with the cattle business.'

Mason considered the boy's support for his companion.

'Glad to hear it, boy,' Mason said offering the newcomer an agreeable nod of accord. 'Now let's get you inside. I guess Mr Johnson here wouldn't say no to a snort of my famous homemade bourbon.'

Lucky accepted the olive branch with a brisk tip of his hat.

It was later that afternoon when the sound of creaking wagon wheels assailed their ears.

'No visitors in a coon's age,' remarked Mason shovelling down a second piece of apple pie, 'and suddenly the Box Bar M has become more popular than a Saturday barn dance.'

All three lurched to their feet and hustled over to the door. The comment might have been light-hearted but Mason still grabbed up his shotgun. On seeing the approaching wagon, he sucked in a deep breath. The wagon was piled high with personal possessions.

A clutch of buzzards wheeled overhead. Settling on the barn roof, they ominously surveyed the proceedings being enacted below.

'That's Lincoln Scarlet and his family,' Mason declared. His face became a darkly solemn mask of rancour. 'Looks like they're pulling out as well.'

He had explained to Lucky the trouble that was brewing in the valley. The wagon rumbled to a grinding halt.

'Some'n bad musta happened to drive you out, Linc,' declared the Box Bar M rancher. A sombre intonation imbued what was a statement rather than a question.

'My two bulls have had their throats cut,' growled the old rancher. His shoulders were slumped, dejection seeping from every pore of his body.

'And they poisoned the well,' added his distraught wife.

'I'm too old for a fight,' mused Scarlet shaking his head. 'And I got the family to think of.'

'So you sold out.' The blunt rejoinder was unintentional in its tone of denouncement. But Howard Mason couldn't contain his anger even though it was aimed at the skunks who were threatening the valley ranchers.

Scarlet was not listening. He had made his decision.

'And you should consider it as well before the same thing happens to the Box Bar M.' Scarlet whipped up the team of four horses and pulled away without voicing any further comment.

'Any notion as to who's behind all this?' Mason called out after the retreating wagon.

Scarlet hauled back on the reins.

'Don't know for certain,' he replied. 'Although I'd put my last dollar on Cody Montaine being at the back of it. That skunk is slippery as an eel.'

Mason concurred with his old friend's inference as he watched the wagon trundling away. His granite face affirmed a grim resolve to sit tight. Nobody was going to drive him out. He would rather die before succumbing to threats and intimidation. He tightened his grip on the Loomis.

Cal slammed a balled fist against the hitching rail. He was equally determined to thwart the skulduggery.

'That pesky varmint ain't no cattle man,' averred Mason furrowing his brow in thought. 'So what's his sneaky game?'

'We're gonna have to band together with the other small outfits for strength in numbers,' suggested Cal. 'The two of us, even with old Jethro helping out, ain't a match for a bunch of hard-boiled gunmen.'

Mason nodded his agreement. 'I'll organize a meeting for tomorrow. Let's just hope none of the others have been *persuaded* to leave.'

Father and son wandered back into the ranch house to formulate their plans.

Had they been watching their guest, they would have perceived him stagger backwards, the blood draining from his face.

Cody Montaine!

Surely there couldn't be two jaspers with that same unusual sobriquet. Some critter must have assumed his identity. As the significance of this abrupt revelation sank in, the missing piece of the puzzle suddenly fell into place. It was like he had just emerged from a dark tunnel into the dazzling brightness of day.

A blinding light of clarification made everything as clear as a church bell. And there imprinted on to his brain was the final piece of the puzzle. The culmination to his eight year quest.

So that was why he had been drawn to Las Vegas.

Reaching into the back pocket of his Levis, Lucky pulled out the faded picture that he had kept all this time. The sepia-tinted image was the only link he had with his enigmatic past.

A youthful Cody Montaine was depicted beside an older gent boasting a thick mane of snow-white hair. The old guy had an affectionate arm slung around his shoulder. They were standing outside a saloon.

On the back was a scrawled message that read, *This will be all yours when I'm pushing up the daisies. Good Luck.* And it was signed: *Trent Buckley.*

He had always pondered on the

identity of the unknown benefactor and what exactly it was that he had inherited. A family friend, grandparent? Maybe even his father.

Now he knew the truth.

Trent Buckley was an uncle on his mother's side. He had died during the war leaving Cody the Red Dragon saloon in Las Vegas, New Mexico. There had been a deed of ownership, but that had gone missing after his attempted murder on Epitaph Ridge. Now he realized that it must have been stolen by the three deadbeats who had gunned him down.

But during the hasty search of his body, they had missed the photograph.

One of the thieving skunks must have come to Las Vegas and claimed the bogus inheritance. And at that very minute he was living the high life as Cody Montaine, owner of the Red Dragon saloon. All he would have needed to do was present the deed of inheritance to a lawyer claiming to be the beneficiary, and the property would have been handed over, no questions asked.

Las Vegas beckoned like a red rag to a bull.

Lucky was seething. His whole being screamed out for revenge. During the eight years in which he had been fumbling about in the dark trying to figure out who he really was, some murdering bastard had taken over his identity. And it looked like he was playing a ruthless game at Cody Montaine's expense.

Quickly he shook off the numbing effects of his discovery.

He would need to maintain the alias of Lucky Johnson until such time as he was in a position to expose the fraud. And that was not going to be easy. Due care and deliberation would need to be exercised to achieve a successful conclusion. Going in with all guns blazing was not an option.

And that would entail keeping these good folks in the dark.

The next day, Lucky Johnson said his

goodbyes. He had offered the services of his guns to the rancher, but Mason was a proud man. No way was he going to bring in hired help of the gunslinging variety. The Gallinas ranchers would handle this in their own way. Even after offering to forego any charge for his services, Mason's stubborn pride stood in the way of accepting any outside help.

'There's six more spreads in this valley,' the stubborn ranch owner emphasized. 'If we all pull together by merging our herds and watching each other's backs, then we can beat that devious Montaine at his own game.'

Hearing his name spat out in the same breath as lowlife vermin was decidedly unsettling. Lucky almost blurted out the truth. His mouth opened. It was Cal Mason that saved him from a course of action he would have regretted. This had to remain a secret until the crooked ne'er-do-well was unmasked and brought to justice.

'I can vouch for Lucky being an OK

guy, Pa,' argued the young man. 'You can't class him as one of those gun-hawks we read about in the newspapers. Those scavengers will do anything for a quick buck. Ain't Lucky proved his worth by refusing any payment?'

But Mason was adamant. His face remained expressionless, blank and inscrutable. He was not to be swayed.

Cal raised his hands in surrender, offering his buddy a look of resignation. 'I tried,' was all he could add as Lucky mounted up.

'Don't forget,' stressed Lucky shaking the ranch owner's hand, 'my help is always available if'n you need it.'

'Much obliged,' replied Mason soft-ening his stoney features. 'No offence meant, but we can fight our own battles in the Gallinas.'

The bounty hunter shrugged. 'None taken. Hope things go your way. Be seeing you.'

Before departing he asked one final question.

'What's the law doing about these

shady takeovers?'

Mason's brittle response was a scornful laugh. 'Charlie Brucker is one of Montaine's lackeys. He got the job when the previous marshal mysteriously disappeared. No one knows where. My guess is that he was ambushed and dumped down some remote canyon for the coyotes to dispose of.'

Once again, Lucky was stunned. He turned his face away to conceal the impact of yet another traumatic jolt. So Mingus Charlie was in Vegas too, and playing at being a lawdog. This was going to be a tougher proposition than he could ever have imagined.

All he could muster was a brief wave of the hand as he rode away.

8

Strength In Numbers

'I asked you boys to come here because we need to do something about these threats to our livelihoods.' Howard Mason was standing on the bed of a wagon inside the barn. 'You all know what I'm talking about.'

He fastened a solemn eye on to the loose gathering. Ranged about in front were a half dozen other ranchers who still had spreads in the Gallinas Valley. Most of them were smaller outfits like the Box Bar M.

The two larger enterprises were run by Ezra Gant of the Flying G and Tug Mackin using the Circle M brand.

Gant was a short beefy dude, red of face and broad as he was tall. The Flying G held much of the land at the top end of the valley and controlled the flow of water running off the Sangre de Cristo range.

There had been trouble with the other ranches when Gant had tried to dam the flow for the purpose of irrigating newly planted crops of squash and corn. The reduced current of water to the rest of the valley had led to legal writs being issued. The matter had only been settled when money had changed hands and Gant agreed to curtail his ambitions for a mixed farming enterprise.

In consequence, tensions had remained high for some months. This was the first time they had all met up since the unfortunate contention which had led to the local cattlemen's association being dissolved. That had enabled unscrupulous elements to move in while the ranchers were in a weakened state.

Gant stood to one side flanked by two of his hands. The ramrod, Trace Elliot, was well known and respected as a top puncher. It was the other jasper, though, who received most attention.

He had a pronounced squint affecting the left eye that gave him a permanent scowl. The guy's hand nervously fingered the bone handle of his pistol. Rondo Swett had only been hired as a wrangler two weeks before.

Tug Macklin scowled across at the Flying G faction. In contrast, he was a lean rangy guy whose angular features ressembled a brooding bald eagle. Most distinctive, however, was a black patch covering his left eye. It had resulted from the stray hoof of a feisty maverick steer that objected to being branded.

Gant was stroking a large Alsatian. The surly hound sensed the antagonism simmering inside the barn. Its mouth drew back in a wicked snarl revealing a full set of lethal ivories. One word and the dog would attack.

There was no love lost between Gant and the others.

Anxious to neutralize the tense atmosphere, Howard raised his voice.

'Any disagreements we've had need to be put aside,' he emphasized trying to cool the prickly mood of the gathering. 'As you are all fully aware, some of the outfits have been forced to accept knockdown terms and as a result have sold up. Nothing that could be proven in a court of law, naturally: poisoned wells, trampled crops and mysterious fires that all followed supposedly innocent land sale offers. One such incident could have been put down as a coincidence.' He scanned the small group of ranchers. 'But not all three.'

Grumbled agreement from Macklin received a curt nod from Gant. The others joined in the angry babble of discord.

'So what you proposin'?' shot back the boss of the Flying G. A rumbling growl from the dog received a swift slap from Gant. The mutt instantly cowered away. It sure knew who was boss. 'I ain't come down here just to be told what we already know. I assume you have some kinda plan worked out?'

'Just coming to that, Ezra,' Mason

calmly assured the impatient rancher. 'My suggestion is that we join our herds together into one large concern. That way we won't be split up into a passel of separate units that can be picked off by these varmints at will.'

'Strength in numbers?' cut in Tug Macklin. 'That what you're sayin, Howie?'

'That's about the size of it,' concurred the spokesman. 'Most of our steers should have been branded by now. So mixing 'em won't matter none. Our boys can then take turns to keep 'em under constant watch while the others look after the ranch buildings.'

He turned his attention to the four smaller outfits. 'My figurin' is that you fellas have been hit first 'cos the skunks clearly reckon you won't put up much of a struggle.'

A sharp eye focused on Gant who had the largest spread. 'But that will only strengthen their hand, give 'em confidence to go for the throat.' The lean smile he aimed at the stocky rancher lacked any hint of mirth. 'Your throat could be next, Ezra, seeing as you have more to lose than any of us.'

Gant's cocky manner dissolved as the implications of Mason's eloquent reasoning sank in. He stroked his stubbly chin in thought.

Mason stood back, arms folded, waiting for the reaction of his associates.

At that moment, Jethro Tate appeared in the doorway with a couple of jugs containing illicit hooch. He was accompanied by Cal Mason who was carrying an array of shot glasses.

His pa was well known in the valley for the quality of his homemade liquor. No saloon grog could touch it for alcoholic strength and taste.

Comments such as, 'It'll blow your head off!' or, 'That stuff kicks harder than a loco mule!' were ample testament to the depth of positive feeling engendered by the Mason Moonshine.

'So what's it to be, boys?' the host rancher pressed. He did not want his guests indulging in a heavy session before they had agreed to his proposal. 'Are you in or out? Stick together and we can end this conniving takeover once and for all.'

Men quietly conversed with one another voicing opinions and seeking accord. One by one they came round to Mason's viewpoint. It all hung on the decision of the Flying G. Without Gant on side, the resistance would lack vigour, be toothless.

All eyes turned towards the smallest man with the largest spread.

This is what Ezra Gant loved, to be the centre of attention. Slowly and with a measured tenor, he lit up a cigar. Blue smoke curled upwards as the rancher milked the occasion to the limit.

'Come on, Gant,' rapped Macklin. 'No need for this play-actin'. Just make up your mind so's we can sample Howard's special brew.' A murmur of accord followed this bluff retort.

'OK, don't get your curlies all tangled up,' huffed Gant enjoying the moment to the full. 'Just considerin' all the options, is all.' He gave a curt nod. 'All right. I'm in, but only until this business is settled.'

Macklin offered the comment a sniff of disdain. 'At last. Now where's that jug?' There followed a surge to where Cal Mason was filling glasses with the potent elixir.

Two hours later, the jugs were empty. The cattle ranchers were reeling. Staggering out of the barn, they wove a tortuous path over to where their cayuses were tethered. Some took more than one attempt to mount up. There were hearty chuckles all round as the unfortunate saps tumbled into the dust.

'Best liquor I ever . . . hic-hic . . . did taste,' observed one slurred voice. The lusty assertion was met with a general yammer of concordance. Even Ezra Gant was in high spirits, as of course were they all, in more ways than one. Tomorrow was soon enough to settle the details of their joint venture to thwart the underhanded land-grab.

'Looks like we brought 'em all round to our way of thinkin', Pa,' declared Cal Mason, polishing off the last drops of the fiery liquor.

'I thought we'd lost Gant though,' said his father. 'That guy sure likes to hog the limelight.'

Cal coughed out a brisk huff of disdain. 'He might be an arrogant cuss, but Ezra Gant ain't no fool. He knows that joining up with the rest of the ranchers is in his best interest.'

Mason nodded in agreement. He was well satisfied with the outcome of the meeting.

Both men were leaning against the barn watching their guests ride off into the afternoon sun. But dark clouds were massing over the mountain tops. In the distance, growls of thunder heralded the approach of a storm. Dust devils swirled around the corral, cavorting in panic.

Roly, their faithful old bloodhound, peeped out of his kennel, his wrinkled features quivering. A fearful keening emerged from the trembling jaws. It was as if he sensed the approach of more than just a turning in the weather. The astute hound clearly felt a more ominous calamity was imminent.

The forewarning passed over the heads of the two Box Bar M men due in no small measure to the liberal effects of Mason's brew. Their elation at the successful outcome of the meeting was icing on the cake.

As the last of the ranchers disappeared from view, Mason slapped his son playfully on the back. Cal winced. His shoulder was healing well, but it would be another week before he could finally shuck the sling.

'Oops!' Mason chided himself. 'Sorry about that, Cal. My patent medicine is stronger than I figured. Makes a fella forget himself.' He chuckled at his own witticism.

A flash of lightning crackled over the serated rim of Truchas Peak to the west. The forked sparkle impinged itself on to the dulled brain of Cal Mason. 'You reckon a storm's on the way, Pa?' he asked.

'Na,' scoffed Mason shaking his head. 'It'll move off north, miss us altogether. You see if'n I ain't right.' An answering grumble of thunder appeared to disagree with the rancher's avowal.

The two men lumbered off back to the ranch house to sleep off the effects of their over-indulgence.

But not all the cattlemen were the worse for wear. One alone among the conclave had ensured that he kept a clear head.

Rondo Swett threw a wary glance towards his employer. They were two miles down the trail from the Mason spread. Gant was rocking in the saddle while humming a tuneless ditty. On his other side, head lolling on his chest, Trace Elliot was almost asleep.

'Any chance of me being allowed to pay a visit to town, boss?' inquired Swett tentatively. 'I found out a couple of days back that an uncle of mine livin' in St Louis has died. Thought I'd arrange some flowers seein' as how I won't make it to the funeral.'

He waited with baited breath for the rancher's response to this singular request. Gant was cantankerous and dour by nature, and not given to benevolent displays of openhandedness. How would he react?

But the power-packed moonshine had mellowed the ranch boss to the point where he was even smiling. On the far side, the ramrod blinked, offering Swett a leery grin.

'Sure, why not,' warbled Gant trying to focus his red-rimmed vision on the speaker. 'A fella should allus show respect to his kinfolks. That's what I say.' Then he leaned over grabbing the wrangler by the arm. 'But make sure to be back by noon tomorrow. Don't forget you got that string of mustangs the army are waitin' on at Fort Union.'

'Much obliged, boss,' sighed the mightily relieved wrangler. 'I won't be late.' He waved a hand eager to be off. 'Be seein' y'all.'

Then he spurred away heading south in the direction of Las Vegas.

His real boss would pay a good bonus for what he'd just learnt.

9

Surprise Encounters

'Scarlet has accepted your offer, Butte.' The speaker handed over an official document. 'And here's the bill of sale signed officially to make it all legal and above board.'

Idaho Black had just burst through the office door.

It was on the upper floor of the Red Dragon saloon in Las Vegas overlooking the town's main street. He was breathing fast, having ridden hard to deliver the anxiously awaited news. Taking off his hat, the burly tough unfastened his red spotted bandanna and wiped it across a sweat-beaded brow.

Black had only arrived in Vegas the previous week. The two old buddies had not crossed paths for two years.

Although initially surprised to see his one-time army confederate, Fresno had put him on the payroll. With Mingus Charlie Brucker installed as town marshal, having Black as support would strengthen his hand considerably.

Instead of congratulating his associate, the saloon owner slammmed a bunched fist down on his desk top. A half empty glass of Scotch jumped into the air splashing the papers he had been perusing. The brown stain went unheeded.

'How many times do I have to say it?' he railed angrily grabbing hold of the land sale and depositing it in the office safe. 'Butte Fresno was laid to rest years ago. I'm Cody Montaine now. One of these days, that big mouth of your'n is gonna spill the beans. And that'll be the end for us all.'

'S-sorry, boss,' whined Black reeling under the verbal onslaught. 'I didn't think.'

'You never do,' Fresno shot back. 'This has gotta remain between the two of us. I've carved out a profitable life for myself out here. And it's all down to that deed of inheritance I took from Sergeant Montaine back on Epitaph Ridge. We both shot him down to escape. Anything comes to light about that and we could both end up dancin' at a rope's end.' He wagged a finger at the sweating confederate. 'You hear me, Idaho? Even the rest of the boys have to be kept in the dark.'

Further discussion of the unsavoury incident was pushed aside as a loud knock sounded on the outside of the door.

'Come in,' rapped Fresno. A heavy-set jasper in dust-caked range garb entered the office. He also had clearly ridden hard.

'Howdie, Rondo,' Fresno greeted the newcomer. 'You seem in an all-fired hurry. Some'n happen I need to know know about?'

'Sure is, boss,' panted the Flying G wrangler. Fresno pushed the bottle across his desk. The cowboy grabbed the neck and sunk a liberal measure before continuing. 'I persuaded Gant to give me the afternoon off. Spun him a tale.'

'How d'yuh manage that?' inquired Black. 'I hear tell Ezra Gant ain't known for bein' the kindhearted sort.'

'Just get to the point,' interjected Fresno impatiently. He had arranged to get Swett installed on the Flying G after learning that the usual wrangler had been killed by a rogue mustang. The big lumbering hardcase was a touch slow-witted but he knew his horseflesh.

Swett imbibed another hefty slug before outlining the events of the afternoon at the Box Bar M ranch.

A grave frown spread across the saloon owner's handsome features. Adjusting his necktie, Fresno gently pulled at the waxed ends of his moustache. It was a trait he effected when tossing over a problem. He only needed to acquire the Box Bar M land for his plans to reach fruition.

But if Gant and the others stepped in

to help out, that could prove a far more difficult endeavour than he had anticipated.

'What we gonna do about it, boss?' asked Swett.

Fresco raised an irritable hand, the waspish regard stifling any further comments. 'Shut up!' he growled, and let me think.'

He stood up and paced the room, eventually reaching a decision.

'This business needs nipping in the bud,' Fresno announced.

A steely glint had replaced the uneasy pallor of minutes before. Nonchalantly, he brushed an imaginary speck of dust from his immaculate dark blue suit.

'The main problem is Mason,' he continued. 'Get rid of him and resistance from the others'll collapse like a house of cards. Gant is no friend of Mason's. Those two have been at loggerheads for months. So he ain't likely to raise much of a stink, especially when you tell him of the gossip you've picked up in town.'

'And what's that, boss?'

'Gant's place ain't in the firing line, is it?' Fresco gave the dim-witted wrangler a supercilious look. Swett's ingenuous features remained blank as the wily gang boss continued. 'Fact is, he can benefit as much as us from this takeover. His land is on the far side of the route planned for the new rail link. So it will more than double it's value.'

'Yeah,' Swett replied, nodding slowly as the drift of the plan began to impinge on to his lethargic brain. 'I see what yuh mean.'

'About time!'

Fresno was about to sketch out the details when there was another knock at the door.

An irritable scowl clouded his features. 'What is it? I'm busy,' he called out with venom.

Gingerly the door opened. It was Tucker Morrison, the bartender.

'Well?' rasped the saloon boss.

'There's a woman here to see you, boss,' stuttered the nervous Morrison.

'Says that you're — '

Fresno testily waved him away cutting the jigger off in mid-flow.

'Tell her to go see Cattle Alice.'

A business associate of Fresno's, Alice, was what could loosely be termed 'A lady of the night'. She ran the local cathouse in which Fresno owned a half share, and had acquired her nickname by accepting animals from cowboys in lieu of cash payment for her services.

'I ain't got time to look her over at the moment.'

The barman persisted. 'This one sure ain't no calico queen, boss,' he stressed. 'She's a lady!' The last word was punched out with vigour. 'Says you're expecting her.'

Expecting a lady? Fresno mouthed the barman's declaration, twisting his face into a series of musing contortions. Who could this mysterious female be? Ladies were a rare feature in Butte Fresno's life. When female companionship was needed, he sent for one of Alice's dames.

Then his eyes widened as remembrance flooded back.

It was while he was in St Louis the previous fall. He'd met this classy chick and they had spent the next week together seeing the sights and enjoying each other's company. Following a particularly amorous night after imbibing too much French wine, he had rashly offered his hand in marriage.

The proposal had come on the night before he was leaving for Las Vegas. It was a spur-of-the-moment notion that a highborn wife would add much needed distinction and refinement to his enterprise.

Their parting had been tearful, on her part at least. He had pledged to send for her as soon as arrangements could be made for her to become his wife.

But like most things in Butte Fresno's life, absence did not make the heart grow fonder. In the cold light of day, it brought regret for having been so cavalier with his vows. Had he really asked a dame to marry him?

And now she had turned up out of the blue. No doubt expecting the honeymoon suite to be ready and waiting.

This required some delaying tactics until such time as he could figure out the best course of action with regard to Miss Felicity Harper. Certainly as he recalled, she was a handsome female and would look good on his arm. The ideal companion for a man heading up in the world.

The men were watching him. Waiting.

'Show her into my living quarters and give her a drink,' Fresno ordered.

'What should I tell her?' replied Morrison.

'Just say I'll be along soon as some business has been sorted out,' he shot back, impatiently waving him away. 'Use your noddle. Ain't that what I'm payin' you for?'

'Yeah, sure, boss,' mumbled the barman backing out of the room.

With his fiancée safely removed from the scene for the time being, Fresno turned his attention back to more important matters.

'Now about this damn troublemaker, Howard Mason,' rasped Fresno beating a clenched fist into the palm of his hand. 'This is how I want it played.'

Ten minutes later, Rondo Swett left to round up three more of Fresno's henchmen to carry out the scurrilous plan to force Howard Mason into submission.

The other man in the office levered himself off the wall.

'What about me . . . Cody?' Black couldn't resist a smirk as he coughed out the appellation. 'Am I not included in this shindig?'

Fresno never noticed the implied slur. 'I got some'n else for you.' He was used to being addressed by his adopted name, and liked it.

After Black had left, Fresno levered off his high boots and swung his long legs up on to the desk. Loosening his necktie, he poured a fresh glass of Scotch and lit up a cigar. And after that, an afternoon with one of Alice's girls. Once this business over the sale of land to the railroad had been completed, he would be set up for life.

Could things get any better?

Then he remembered. The serene look of pleasure dissolved like sugar in a coffee cup. He now had a fiancée to contend with.

* * *

Lucky Johnson was making his way to Las Vegas. The trail paralleled the Sangre de Cristos mountains. It was an undulating trail that meandered between surging pinacles of orange sandstone. Blunt fingers of rock pointed to the cloudless sky.

He had just crested a low knoll when a puff of yellow dust a mile ahead caught his attention. It must be another rider coming his way. Always cautious when encountering other travellers, especially on lonely trails, Lucky drew his mount into the cover of a clump of ponderosa pine trees. Once the jasper passed, he would continue on his way.

He did not have long to wait. The gentle thrum of trotting hoofs announced the approach of the rider. Peering out, Lucky watched the traveller draw near.

Even from a distance where facial identification was impossible, Lucky instantly recognized the hated profile of Idaho Black. Now was his chance to get the drop on the elusive varmint. He hauled out his rifle and jacked a round up the spout ready to confront the outlaw.

Then a notion occurred to him. What was he doing out here, and heading in the opposite direction from Las Vegas?

Maybe he should follow and ascertain what Black was up to.

The outlaw passed Lucky's place of concealment, totally unaware that he was being eyeballed. Keeping the outlaw in view, Lucky dogged his trail all the way to the town of Watrous.

It was late afternoon. Black tied up outside the Golden Nugget Hotel, went inside and booked himself a room. His intention was to collect the store rents from those properties owned by Fresno the following morning and get back to Vegas by nightfall.

Lucky gave him chance to settle down before he entered the hotel. Ambling casually up to the reception desk, he slapped a ten dollar bill under the nose of the clerk and said, 'A guy just booked a room. What number is he in?' A hard flinty gaze pinned the little man to the spot. 'There'll be another of these coming your way if'n you're still here when I come back down.'

Beads of sweat broke out on the clerk's bald pate. He knew a gunslinger when he saw one.

'A f-friend of y-your'n?' stammered the guy pointing to an empty key ring numbered five.

'We're acquainted,' came back the brisk retort.

Lucky flashed another tenner in front

of the trembling clerk's face, then disappeared up the staircase. Half way up, he paused and turned, a forefinger placed across his grinning mouth. The clerk gave a vigorous nod of understanding.

At the top of the stairs was a corridor. A strip of threadbare carpet enabled him to approach room number five in silence. It was located at the end of the passage where a window overlooked the main street.

Lucky continued past the door and hauled up the window sash. It faced on to a fenced veranda. And just around to his right was the window belonging to room five. A satisfied smiled played across the gaunt features.

Returning to Black's room, he withdrew the wanted dodger from his pocket and smoothed it out. Bending down, he slid it under the door, then knocked three times.

A puzzled grunt from inside the room was enough to inform the hunter that the paper had been noted. There followed a twanging of springs as Black got up off the bed where he had been reclining. Quick as a flash, Lucky cat-footed to the end window and stepped through out on to the veranda.

In the street below, wagons passed and people went about their normal business. Nobody had noticed the deadly game being conducted in their midst. Only a lone buzzard perched on the roof opposite seemed to be displaying any interest.

Gliding towards the room window, he heaved a thankful sigh that the lower sash was fully raised. That made his task all the easier. Quickly he peered inside.

Black was staring at the poster. Seconds passed as the full significance struck home. An ugly growl erupted from his mouth as he hauled out his gun and triggered off three shots. The bullets splintered the door at chest height slamming into the corridor wall opposite.

All of the outlaw's attention was

focused on the door.

A single step and Lucky was inside the room.

'Don't move a muscle, Idaho,' he spat, jabbing his own pistol at the stunned outlaw's back. 'This time you've been nabbed. Now drop that hogleg and turn around slow and easy.'

Reluctantly, Black complied. He had no choice.

Lucky faced his old adversary head on.

'Now take a good look,' he said, 'and tell me who you see.'

Black's eyes opened wide. 'You again.' He still hadn't recognized his old sergeant. 'I should have gunned you down when I had the chance.'

'Look closer, Idaho.' Lucky smiled, tapping his grey hat. 'Remember Epitaph Ridge, do yuh?'

For a moment the outlaw's face remained blank, a flat expression of puzzlement dulling his brain. Then the penny dropped. Beady eyes widened, almost popping out of his head. A wavering finger pointed. Blood drained from the skeletal face like he'd seen a ghost.

'You're s-supposed to be d-dead,' he stuttered. He shook his head. 'Am I in hell?'

An ugly snarl rent the fetid air as Lucky grabbed hold of Black's greasy hair and flung him on to the bed. The snout of his revolver bit deep into the outlaw's ear.

'You soon will be, ratface.'

The gun twisted. The ominous click of the hammer snapping to full cock heralded an imminent trip south to the fiery furnace for Idaho Black. Lucky's trigger finger blanched white.

'Hold up there,' said Black, his voice cracking in panic. 'What d'yuh want me to do? Just say the word. It's Fresno you really want. He's the one that stole your inheritance. I can give you the lowdown on his plans.'

The tense finger slackened momentarily. It was true. The termination of Butte Fresno was his primary concern.

'OK, Black,' Lucky growled. 'You've earned a reprieve. That is, so long as I like what you have to spill.'

'Sure, sure, Sergeant,' burbled the quaking outlaw. 'Anything you say. Just slack up a mite with that trigger finger. It's makin' me nervous. And I don't think straight when I get edgy.'

Lucky snarled, flung the outlaw on to his back across the bed and jammed the pistol's hard barrel up the jigger's mashed snout.

'I don't give a plugged nickel about your feelings,' he ranted. 'Just tell me what Fresno's up to and I'll think about letting you off the hook. Now talk. And it better be good.'

Black told all.

How Fresno had conned the local lawyer into ratifying ownership of the Red Dragon; his branching out into other lucrative enterprises. Most significant for the immediate future was the forcible eviction of settlers off land in the Gallinas Valley at derisory prices. Armed with official bills of sale, it had been easy for the devious skunk to claim ownership himself once his minions had done their work.

Next it was Lucky's turn to register surprise when Black revealed that Fresno's aim was to sell the land to the Denver Rio Grande Railroad Company. They wanted to connect the current line to the Atchison Topeka at Santa Fe. Use of the Gallinas Valley would obviate the need for an expensive detour to the east.

Butte Fresno had seen an opportunity to make a lot of dough. The moral implications of his highhandedly callous methods cut no ice with the ruthless brigand. Any notion of fair play was like water off a duck's back. And as long as he was paying the wages, his hard-bitten crew would carry out the ruthless skunk's bidding.

Worst of all, as far as the bounty hunter was concerned, was that he would receive all the condemnation. Once Fresno had pocketed his ill-gotten gains and quit the territory, the good name of Cody Montaine would be dirt in the eyes of those left behind to pick up the pieces.

When Black had finished, Lucky needed all his concentration to mull over the undertones. It was a lot to take in. Keeping his eye on the hovering outlaw, he posed one final question.

'So when is Fresno planning to do the dirty on the ranchers who are left?'

'Tomorrow,' was the emphatic response. 'And he'll be takin' the short cut through Buckskin Gap.' Black waited a moment while his adversary ruminated on what needed to be done. 'So am I free to go?' he inquired gingerly edging slowly towards the door.

Lucky gave a peremptory nod of accord.

'But if'n I see your mangy hide again,' he rasped out, 'I'll feed it to the buzzards.'

Black's thin lips split to emit a rancid growl. But the grim expression of vengeance on Lucky's granite face made him think better of it. So he remained silent. He bent down to retrieve his gun.

'Leave it!' rapped the hunter.

A moment's hesitation, then Black picked up his bedroll and saddle-bags and moved to the door.

Lucky turned away, holstering his gun. He peered around searching for his hat which had been knocked off while entering the room through the veranda window. When Black saw that his nemesis had been distracted, he sensed an opportunity to turn the tables.

Gingerly he stooped down and took hold of the fallen revolver. The gun rose, then swung towards the unprotected back of Lucky Johnson.

But Lucky had already figured that given the chance his old adversary would pull such a devious stunt. A leopard never changes its spots. And varmints like Idaho Black were crooked to the core.

So he was ready.

Black had failed to see that Lucky

was watching his every move through the small mirror pinned to the wall. Not giving the outlaw the chance to haul back the hammer, he spun and let fly with both barrels of the tiny derringer he had recently acquired.

The treacherous outlaw's mouth opened in total shock at this unexpected reversal of fortune.

He reeled back against the wall and slid to the floor, a trail of smeared red in his wake. Derringers might not be useful in the open, but they were lethal at close range. Lucky Johnson gave thanks to the Reverend Amos Farrow for that vital piece of advice.

'You were given the chance, mister,' observed the hunter in a flat monotone voice. 'And you blew it.'

Black's glassy eyes flickered once before his head fell forward. His killer spat on the bleeding corpse, the hard face remaining inscrutable. There had been no pleasure gained from the killing. Even the hefty reward due did not raise a smile. Only a deep-rooted satisfaction that justice had been meted out.

But already his thoughts were moving towards finding a solution to the dilemma raised by Black's confession regarding Butte Fresno's objectives. He would need to move fast if a catastrophe was to be avoided.

10

Buckskin Gap

'Rider coming in, Pa,' called out a disquieted Cal Mason. 'Looks like he's alone and in one heck of a rush.'

A keen breeze stirring up the dry sand was further agitated by pounding hoofs. It enveloped the newcomer making identification impossible.

Cal grabbed a rifle and poked it through the window of the log cabin. Meanwhile, the older man stepped outside, a shotgun held at the ready. Not until the rider had entered the corral was he able to recognize the bounty hunter.

Wrestling the charging horse to a halt, Lucky leapt from the saddle.

'Looks like I got here in time,' he spluttered sucking in lungfuls of air. 'I've ridden non-stop from Watrous to tell you . . . ' He paused. Snatching up a dipper of water from a bucket, he took a long drink.

'Tell me what?' posed the baffled rancher.

'Just let me feed and water the cayuse then I'll fill you in.'

Although impatient to hear what he assumed was disturbing news, the rancher nodded towards the barn.

'Go see Jethro. He'll look after the mare. Then come over to the house when you're done. We can open a fresh jug.' Mason lowered the shotgun. A worried frown pursued the sweat-stained back of the mysterious bounty hunter.

'What d'yuh suppose it's all about?' inquired his equally bewildered son, who had joined him outside on the veranda.

Mason shrugged. 'Judging by the grim look on his face, it can't be anything good.' He turned away. 'Come on. I think we both need a drink.'

Ten minutes later, Lucky joined them.

He tipped up the heavy earthenware jug and took a drink of the potent brew. The fiery tipple burned down his throat, warming his innards and precipitating a shiver of euphoria through his tired body. He emitted a low whistle of appreciation.

'Wow!' he exclaimed refusing another slug. 'That stuff sure hits the mark. But we're gonna need all our senses clear and steady if Fresno and his gang are gonna be outwitted.'

Mason screwed his features into a bewildered grimace. 'Who in tarnation is this Fresno character? Never heard the name before.'

'You'll know him as Cody Montaine,' Lucky explained with pointed deliberation. He paused before continuing. 'But I'm the real Montaine. Butte Fresno stole my identity.'

Both father and son looked askance at this unexpected disclosure.

'I think you've gotten some explaining to do,' elicited Mason, taking a hefty swig of moonshine. 'Comin' out with a claim like that, calm as you please, is apt to juggle a man's brain.'

Lucky nodded. 'Guess it is a lot to take in,' he agreed. 'Maybe I do need another slug.' He tipped the jug and imbibed a fresh belt before spelling out his accusations.

'The jasper you know as Cody Montaine is in cahoots with two bushwacking sidekicks who left me for dead during the last days of the war. They also stole my inheritance and then came out west to claim it in my name.' A lurid scowl creased the hunter's face. 'I caught up with one of them yesterday.' He turned to address Cal Mason. 'It was Idaho Black, that skunk who tried to rob the stage. He'd joined up with his old buddy in Las Vegas. Well he won't be doing any more thieving. And that's a certainty.'

He didn't need to elucidate.

Lucky then went on to quickly fill the two ranchers in on the details of his life since being dragged back from the brink on Epitaph Ridge.

Once he had finished, it took some minutes for the full significance of the revelation to sink in. Mason puffed furiously on his corncob pipe while his son paced the room digesting the remarkable particulars of his *compadre's* divulgence.

'Man, that's some tale,' ejaculated Howard Mason, shaking his head. 'I can see now why you wanted to keep your true identity under cover.'

'The main thing,' Cody hurried on, 'is that Fresno has you down as the ringleader of the ranchers. He's planted a spy with Ezra Gant. It was him that spilled the beans about your meeting and what you intended doing to thwart his plans to gain control of the Gallinas Valley.'

'And his crew are coming here to burn us out, you say?'

Cody nodded adding in a sombre tone, 'And likely make certain they get you both out of the way permanently.'

Mason was nonplussed. 'What we

166

gonna do?' His voice was plaintive, devoid of anger or feeling. Normally a resilient and uncompromising fighter when it came to defending his rights, this news had knocked the stuffing out of him.

His son placed a comforting arm around the drooping shoulders.

'Don't worry, Pa,' he soothed trying ineffectually to ease the big man's trauma. 'We'll show these lowdown skunks that the Masons ain't no easy pushovers.'

But it was Cody who took charge of the problem.

'According to Black, Fresno's gang will make their move today.' In the half-light cast by the flickering oil lamp, his angular features were set like stone. 'They're heading this way right now. That's why I was in such a darned hurry to get here. So there ain't a moment to lose if'n we're gonna do some'n about stopping them.'

'How we gonna do that?' asked young Mason.

'We have the advantage of knowing in advance what their intentions are, right?' posed Cody in a slow orderly voice.

Cal nodded, waiting.

'So if we can somehow turn the tables on them . . . ' he paused, thinking. The bounty hunter grunted to himself, his tight jaw moving silently in furiously concentrated thought.

Nobody spoke. Two pairs of earnest peepers were glued to his stoic, earnest expresion.

Finally Cody Montaine put his deliberations into words. His voice held a note of sanguinity that even had the disconsolate Howard Mason paying attention.

'Jethro looks too old for this sort of caper,' he said. 'So that leaves the three of us against . . . ' he shrugged unknowingly. 'Maybe six or more, who knows. We need to stop them at a place where a small group will have the upper hand. Black told me that they intend coming through a place called Buckskin

Gap. Do you know it?'

Howard Mason's face lit up.

'If they're coming through the Gap, we have a good chance of giving them a hot reception.' His voice had regained some of its fire. A glimmer of the old spirit that had been instrumental in helping the rancher to tame this wild country was reflected in the fervid gaze. 'One man and a rifle could hold an army at bay there.'

'How far is it?' asked Cody.

'No more than an hour's ride,' came back the avid response.

'Then what we waiting for?' Cody stressed, heading for the door. 'There ain't a moment to lose.'

Urged on by the hunter's impassioned manner, they hurried outside and quickly saddled up. Guns were checked and extra ammunition stuffed into saddle-bags.

'Keep your eyes peeled, Jethro,' Mason warned his long-time hand accepting a parcel of fresh-cut beef sandwiches. 'Just in case those varmints get by us. But don't do anything rash. Your mangy old carcass is too valuable to lose, hear me?' There was genuine affection in the gruff comment.

Jethro Tate had just appeared one day when Mason was setting up the ranch. A drifter, cut loose when the Texas ranch of Charles Goodnight had amalgamated with that of Oliver Loving, he had headed north intending to find work on one of the New Mexico outfits in the Pecos Valley.

Howard Mason had offered him some temporary work cutting logs and help with the construction of the new ranch in exchange for vittles and a bed of straw.

Initially just passing through, he had stayed on. That had been six years before. Jethro's culinary skills had been much appreciated by the new rancher. And since then, they had attracted almost as much acclaim as the renowned Box Bar M moonshine.

But not quite.

'Don't you worry, boss,' opined the

oldster gripping his ancient Hawken. 'My hide is tougher than an overcooked rib-eye. Ain't no bullets gonna get through this.' He jabbed a gnarled finger at his hollow chest.

With a cheery wave, Mason led the way as they spurred off towards the line of bluffs on the horizon to the south. Time was now of the essence if they were to thwart the land grabbers.

*　*　*

They found a suitable place to observe any approaching riders. And there they settled down, concealed in the cluster of boulders near to where Buckskin Gap opened out on to the plains.

The unusual rift was a weakness in the impenetrable sandstone cliffs that had been eroded over time by wind and water. Inside the eroded split, sheer walls of rock rising up on either side were shrouded in perpetual shadow. Where no light could penetrate, even the ubiquitous sagebrush and mesquite were absent.

At certain points, the overhang was so pronounced that a man could jump from one side to the other. In consequence, horses were forced into single file along much of its tortuous course. That was especially the case as the exit was neared.

It thus offered the ideal position to launch an attack.

Unable to retreat, the gang would be at their mercy.

Once they had settled into their respective positions, the three men waited. An hour passed with still no sign of the gang.

Mason was getting restive.

'Where in thunder are those blasted varmints?' he railed impotently. 'They should have been here by now.'

'Is there no other way of reaching Box Bar M from Las Vegas?' inquired Cody.

'Not unless they take the main trail through Wagon Mound Pass,' growled

Mason. 'But that's adding another four hours to their journey.' His tone betrayed a frustrating doubt. 'Could they have taken the longer route, d'yuh reckon?' It was a question to which the other two ambushers lacked any answer.

'You certain it was Buckskin Gap that Black mentioned?' asked a worried Cal Mason.

Cody lifted his shoulders in confirmation as he glanced at the sky.

The afternoon sun had disappeared over the western rim of the mountains. Another couple of hours and dusk would be ushering in the onset of darkness. It was no time to be setting an ambush.

The lengthening shadows matched Cody's mood.

That itch on the back of his neck was giving him a bad feeling about this business. The more he thought about it, the more ominous were his conclusions regarding Idaho Black's disclosures. The outlaw had been somewhat over eager in passing on vital information concerning the impending showdown.

At the time Cody's own delight at learning of the attack had overshadowed any doubts regarding the varmint's veracity. Had Black deliberately led him up a blind alley knowing that his old sergeant was going to let him off the hook if'n he spilled the beans?

The itch was becoming more pronounced by the second.

Inwardly he berated himself for having been suckered. Black had suffered the ultimate penalty for his treachery. But that was no compensation.

He threw a wary glance at his confederates. Both sets of eyes were fixed on the narrow ravine. Cody was relieved that the guilt clearly displayed across his lean face went unnoticed. No way was he about to admit to having been duped. Cody Montaine had his professional pride. All he could do now was try to put things right.

'Don't reckon they'll come now,' he averred standing up. 'Best we get back to the ranch and wait on 'em there.'

Mason nodded reluctantly. He was also becoming suspicious that they might have been tricked.

11

A Shock For Cody

The three men rode in silence.

Their individual thoughts were focused on what they might find back at the ranch. Twittering meadowlarks went unheeded; prairie dogs capering playfully above their burrows were ignored. Stiff-backed, hands tightly gripping the reins, they galloped onward at a frenetic speed.

Faces were set hard as iron.

The urgency of their fears communicated itself to the horses who lengthened their pace accordingly.

Even before the ranch came in sight, it became clear that they had been hoodwinked. Swirling coils of smoke drifting above the distant line of low hills did not originate from any campfire. Vengeance and a blazing firebrand had come to the Box Bar M.

Cresting a low rise overlooking the cluster of buildings, the hair-raising scene drew gasps of horror from father and son.

The main cabin had been reduced to ashes. Blackened timbers poked through the drifting curtain of smoke like accusing fingers of doom. Only the barn had survived.

But more heart-rending was the sight of Jethro Tate lying face down in the dirt. A dark stain around the body was enough to inform the riders that the old timer would not be making any more of his renowned son-of-a-gun stew.

Howard Mason surrendered to a paroxysm of grief.

Leaping from his horse, he bent down and hugged the shattered corpse to his chest. Tears of abject sorrow mingled with the lifeforce of his old buddy.

'At least the old boy got one of the bastards before he was cut down,' snarled Cal Mason toeing the corpse on to its back. 'And look who it was!' The identity of the dead arsonist came as a surprise to the young puncher. 'None other than that treacherous snake, Rondo Swett, the double-dealing toad who worked for Gant.'

Wracked with guilt, Cody's head sunk on to his chest.

'If'n I hadn't been taken in by Black's eagerness to blow the whistle, we might have been able to prevent this. The entire caboodle was nought but a pack of lies.' Shuffling his feet, shame enveloped the bounty hunter in its cloying grip. 'I oughtn't to have been such a dumb jackass in believing his chicanery. Especially after he tried to jump me.'

'It ain't your fault, Cody,' mollified Cal Mason trying to save his old partner's face. 'How were you to know he was playing with loaded dice?'

Howard Mason was too wracked with grief to care. But the rancher was not one to allow such a setback to dog him for long.

Carefully and with due reverence, he laid his buddy down and stood up. Slumped shoulders straightened. An ugly grimace had replaced the woeful look of despair. For the first time since he had witnessed the destruction of his property, the rancher gave vent to his feelings.

Nobody interrupted the painful outpouring of grief and hatred for the perpetrators. Finally he ran out of expletives regarding the ancestry of Butte Fresno. Gasping for breath, he lumbered over to what had been the front door and stepped into the ruins of his home.

Neither of the other two followed. Howard Mason needed to be alone. He emerged some ten minutes later clutching a jug of moonshine.

'Let's drink a toast, boys,' he rasped handing out cracked mugs and splashing the strong liquor into them. A twisted grin pasted across the wrinkled features held no trace of levity. Then, raising the jug into the still air, he continued in a voice raspy and crackling with emotion. 'To the memory of old friends . . . ' He took a drink before snarling out the rest of the toast. 'And the death of hated enemies.'

The declaration was measured and with no hint of rancour. It was as if he was just passing the time of day.

But the dour expresson, grim and resolute, left no doubts of the vengeful resolve to be exacted. Full retribution would be exacted for the heinous despoilation of his life's endeavour.

'So what we waiting for?'

Mason hustled across to his horse, intent on carrying out his promise.

However, Cody Montaine had other ideas.

The bounty hunter had the same resolve, albeit for different reasons. But saddling himself with an ageing rancher was not part of his plan to rid the world of Butte Fresno and restore his good name. Apart from that one time he had taken on Cal Mason as a partner, the bounty hunter had always worked alone. He much preferred it that way.

And this time was no different.

'Hold on there, Howard,' he said stepping forward and holding the reins tightly. 'Ain't no sense in going off half-cocked without a plan of action. This thing needs thinking out if'n we're to destroy Fresno's devious scheme.' His firm gaze held that of the stubborn rancher. 'And you are needed here.'

Mason tried to push past him.

'What d'yuh mean?' he blustered. 'I ain't about to stand by and allow that lowdown piece of dung to ride rough-shod over me.'

Cody held his ground. 'Nobody's asking you to. But you're a rancher, not a gunslinger. That's my business, remember?' He didn't wait for a response. 'You need to bury poor old Jethro and rally the other spreads ready for a fight if'n the need arises. What you agreed with Gant and the others still stands. Hopefully it won't come to a confrontation if my plan works out.'

Mason's eyes widened. 'You gotten

some'n' in mind?'

Cody nodded. 'Best to keep it under wraps until I've sorted out the details. Main thing is you stay here while me and Cal go into Las Vegas and he brings the sheriff out here to investigate the fire.'

'What darned good will that do?' railed the impatient rancher, not yet convinced of his confederate's optimistic manner.

'Mingus Charlie Brucker is one of Fresno's men,' Cody persisted. 'Once we've got the varmint out here, you and the other boys can hold him prisoner. That'll leave the way open for me to deal with Fresno unhindered by any so-called legal interference. What d'yuh say? Is it a deal?'

He held out a hand expectantly.

Mason was still not fully persuaded. He huffed some trying to think up objections to being left behind. It was his son who rallied support for the bounty hunter's proposal.

'Sounds good to me, Pa,' he enthused.

'I don't want you getting shot up by a bunch of hard-bitten gunmen. This way, you can get the others together. Then it'll be strength in numbers. Even Gant will give his support once he discovers that his wrangler was nought but a stinking Judas.'

'Guess you're right,' Mason finally acknowledged, although still rather disappointed that he was not included in the action. 'I'll bury poor old Jethro next to Millie in the orchard.' His head bowed at the thought of his deceased wife. 'Then ride over to see Tug Macklin. He can spread the word while I go see Gant.'

*   *   *

Cody spent the night in the barn. It was a restless few hours. Images of those haunting final minutes on Epitaph Ridge refused to go away. He must have dropped off at some point because the crowing of the rooster had jerked his fermenting brain back to the present.

Following a makeshift breakfast of beans and tortillas prepared by Cal Mason and washed down with strong coffee, they were ready to go.

'You boys take care,' stressed a deeply concerned Howard Mason. 'The two of you agin that bunch of skunks ain't good odds.'

Cody gave the rancher a reassuring smile. 'You worry too much, Howard,' he averred, confidence oozing from every pore. 'I've come up against critters like Fresno before. I'll soon have his goose cooked.'

But riding out of the corral alongside Cal Mason, he still had not come up with a way of thwarting his deadly rival. All he knew for certain was that Butte Fresno had to be removed from the scene in such a way as to discredit his rectitude with the town council and the railway company.

Cut off the snake's head and the body would wither and die. Put another way, remove the bossman who paid the wages and the hired help would disappear back into the ratholes from whence they emerged.

Only by proving to those in authority that Fresno was a crook and a charlatan could he hope to pick up his life and start afresh.

It was mid afternoon when the two riders came in sight of Las Vegas. Cody drew to a halt.

'You know what to do,' he said to Cal Mason, his grimly austere features relaxing into a sympathetic regard. 'Lay on the grief with a thick trowel. It shouldn't be difficult under the circumstances. But you need to get Brucker out of town.' The hard look reasserted itself. 'I'll deal with him later.'

'I won't let you down, Cody.'

They shook hands as the younger man nudged his horse along the well-worn trail towards the outer fringe of the town. Tall stands of yucca on either side swayed in greeting, like some primeval welcoming committee.

Cody watched until he disappeared from view before moving off the trail along a shallow draw. He had no wish to enter Las Vegas until Mingus Charlie had left with his partner.

Once out of sight and shielded by a rocky outcrop, the bounty hunter made camp. Settling down, he waited for nightfall.

★   ★   ★

Yellow light cast by innumerable oil lamps flickered as Cody Montaine hugged one side of Las Vegas's main street. A heavy sigh of relief escaped from between pursed lips when he saw that the sheriff's office was in darkness.

An owl hooted in greeting. In the distance, the mournful keening of a lone coyote lent an eerie feeling to the rider's progress up the busy street.

Two blocks down from the Red Dragon saloon, he stopped. Dismounting, he tied off. Nobody paid the newcomer any heed. Just as he liked it. With pantherlike ease, he move along the boardwalk, sharp eyes glued to the batwing doors of the saloon. Automatically he slipped the trigger thong, loosening the revolver in its cross-draw holster.

Almost opposite the saloon, he stopped and lit up a cheroot. Blue smoke twined in the still air as he studied the saloon, figuring out how to make his move. Finally having come to a decision that a direct approach was best, he stepped forward to cross the street.

At that moment, two people emerged from the saloon, a man and a woman. The woman leaned up and kissed the man on the lips. It was a moment of tender affection that found Cody Montaine struggling to remain upright. The blood drained from his face. He felt decidedly faint. His mouth flapped open.

The two people separated.

Butte Fresno headed off in one direction while the girl crossed the street heading towards where Cody was standing.

It was Felicity Harper. The numbing

realization that this winsome creature was engaged to his hated enemy was like a kick in the guts from a rodeo mustang.

Cody was stunned into immobility. His legs threatened to give way.

Needing time to rally his frazzled mind, Cody managed to draw back into the shadows. He was grateful that the moon chose that moment to scuttle behind a balloon of cloud, its ethereal glow muted.

Miss Harper passed by within feet of the hidden watcher unaware of his presence. His eyes followed her passage to the Palace Hotel. At least she had not yet tied the knot. Although judging by the pair's amorous parting, that could only be a matter of time.

Cody snarled. His fists clenched, the knuckles blanching in wrathful fury. Yet at the same time he felt impotent. Any frontal assault on his enemy's redoubt was now abandoned. All he could think of was persuading Miss Harper as to the dire consequences of entering into a permanent liaison with a lowlife of Butte Fresno's ilk.

The thought made his whole body shudder.

After making inquiries as to the lady's room number, Cody gingerly mounted the stairs to the upper floor.

He paused outside her room, fist raised ready to knock on the door. Hesitation stayed his next move. How could he prevail upon a woman so clearly besotted that her paramour was a cheating murderous coward?

But what other choice did he have, being equally smitten?

He rapped on the door.

'Who's there?' called out the dulcet tones from within.

A pause as Cody swallowed. He was more nervous than a greenhorn kid on his first date.

Again.

'Is anyone there?'

He coughed to hide the nervous croak in his throat. 'It's Mr Mo . . ' he almost said Montaine having gotten so used to his real appendage in recent days. 'It's Mr Johnson, Lucky Johnson, ma'am. We met on the Santa Fe Stage,' he replied. 'You said to call on you if I was ever in Las Vegas.'

A shuffling followed this announcement. Then the door was opened. And there she stood, just as beautiful as he remembered. Maybe even more so.

'What a pleasant surprise, Mr Johnson.' Her radiant smile transformed the dimly lit room. 'Please come in.'

Clutching his hat, Cody stepped inside. He sucked in a deep lungful of air. This was no time for idle chitchat. He was here to deliver bad news. Best to get it over and done with.

'I need to ask you, Miss Harper, what exactly you know about this guy Cody Montaine?' He swallowed hard. 'Where did you meet?'

The young woman immediately sensed the negative aura pulsating from her visitor. She frowned, drawing back from his outstretched hand.

'Why do you ask that?' she mur-mured, clearly unsettled by this foray into her personal affairs. Then in a more brusque tone, added, 'and what business is that of yours?'

Cody shuffled under the girl's caustic gaze. Maybe he should have ap-proached this with more decorum. Too late now. Another deep breath.

'Because I'm the real Cody Mon-taine,' he blustered, eager to get it all out in the open. 'That jasper you're engaged to marry is Butte Fresno, an army deserter who shot me down and stole my identity, not to mention my inheritance.'

Not stopping, he hurried on to briefly outline the whole sorry episode. He paused in mid-flow, eyes silently imploring her to believe him. Before he could continue the diatribe, she held up a hand.

'Stop right there!' Her tone was bluntly incisive. 'How dare you come in here denigrating my fiancé. If I didn't know better, I would say you were jealous of his success and have come here with the sole intention of besmirching his good name.'

'No, ma'am!' exclaimed Cody. 'It ain't like that at all. I'm telling you the goldarned truth. Fresno is a swindler who's out to grab all the land around here by fair means or foul. He's already forced out some of the ranchers and is out to eject the rest, legally or otherwise.'

'And what proof have you to back up these wild accusations?' The sneering inflection was a direct challenge. And it originated from a woman who was prepared to fight tooth and nail for the man for whom she had given up much. Hands firmly resting on swaying hips, she stood her ground, waiting.

All she expected were sob-story words, nothing concrete to support such a bizarre claim.

Much as Cody was determined to meet that challenge, his heart was heavy with remorse. He resented Fresno all the more for making him the heel that this woman now regarded with loathing. But there was no choice. Hopefully when she learned the truth about her beloved, new bridges could be built.

Slowly he removed the photograph from his jacket, the one showing Cody Montaine as a much younger man outside the Red Dragon saloon. He showed it to the girl.

'That's me with my uncle, Trent Buckley. He was my ma's brother.'

Felicity scanned the sepia tint briefly, then shrugged. 'What is this meant to prove?'

'That signature.' He jabbed a finger at the scrawled writing. 'It oughta match the one on the document held by Fresno. If it does, wouldn't that prove I'm telling the truth that your fiancé stole my identity and good name to inherit what is rightfully mine? More important than any of that,' he held the girl with an appealing regard, 'is that his low-down deception stole your heart. For that he can never be forgiven.'

The girl's face reddened, softened

momentarily, before once again assuming a caustic frown registering scepticism.

Again she perused the photograph, this time more carefully. Confusion began to dapple the alabaster complexion. Could it possibly be true what this mysterious stranger was trying to have her believe? He certainly wove a convincing story. Yet such insinuations seemed so far-fetched. Surely if her betrothed was lying, she would have known. A woman's intuition. She turned away to hide her vacillation.

Cody sensed the girl's indecision and pressed home his case.

'If you could get hold of that inheritance document and verify the two signatures were written by the same person, surely that would prove beyond doubt that I am telling the truth. Then this whole sorry business can be brought out into the open.'

Cody silently urged the girl towards his point of view. But he dared not say more for fear of overplaying his hand. It was up to her now.

After what seemed like a lifetime, Felicity Harper announced her decision.

'Meet me here at the same time tomorrow. I'll let you know then what I have managed to find out . . . if anything.'

Cody had to be satisfied with that.

'I'll be here,' he said shuffling over to the door. 'But promise me you'll be careful. That varmint is dangerous. Him and his bunch shot me down and left me for dead on the battlefield. Then they deserted. It's taken me eight years to catch up with Butte Fresno.' He paused, fixing Miss Harper with a determined eye. 'You're my only hope of making sure that justice prevails.'

The girl gave the tetchy comment an imperious sniff. She was still not convinced that the man she had intended to marry was such a blackguard. It was as well, therefore, that Cody failed to witness her doubts regarding the bounty hunter's claim as he left the room.

With a renewed sense of anticipation that his quest was nearing its fulfillment, he headed back to his campsite outside the town limits.

12

Out Of The Frying Pan . . .

A troubled frown creased the alluring contours of Felicity Harper's winsome visage as her gaze followed the enigmatic stranger's exit from Las Vegas. Still unable to fully accept his emphatic accusations concerning her fiancé, nevertheless, doubts were setting in.

Gone were the rose-tinted images of passionate love held when she first arrived. Frontier life was especially tough for women. Luxuries she had taken for granted in the big city were sorely lacking. Life was much more rough and ready.

And her fiancé was no longer the attentive suitor he had been when they first met. He always seemed too busy to pay her the attention she craved. But there were other things niggling at her mind. Nothing too obvious, but doubts just the same. Things that only now were beginning to question her commitment to the saloon owner.

It had taken the arrival of Lucky Johnson, who now claimed to be the real Cody Montaine, to bring them to the fore.

How her fiancé always clammed up when she entered a room; the dissolute array of hard-bitten toughs who were always around. The lascivious attention she had secretly witnessed that he paid to new dancers arriving at the saloon. When challenged, he had, of course, vehemently denied any impropriety. It was all just harmless fun that meant nothing.

Most disturbing, however, was the fact that he had thus far refused to name a date for the wedding. It was always deferred to a later date when business was less hectic. Excuses? Or had he changed his mind?

Again, concerned eyes swivelled to the disappearing rider. Could his accusations be true?

Still undecided, Felicity Harper moved away from the window and slumped down on to her bed. She needed time to think. Perhaps a good night's sleep would help clear her confused thoughts.

Following a disturbed night, she rose early. Crossing to the window, she peered out at the busy street below.

Wagons containing all manner of goods trundled past. The crack of a whip heralded the arrival of the stage from Santa Fe. From the west, a herd of steaming longhorns were being pushed towards their holding pens on the edge of town. The girl dabbed a scented lace handkerchief to her nose to disguise the rank odour of the lowing cattle.

Their offensive passage down the middle of the street was forgotten when she perceived Butte Fresno emerging from the dark interior of the Red Dragon saloon. He was alone and looking quite shifty. Furtively peering up and down the street, he then mounted up and spurred off. Leaning out of the window, Felicity could see that he was headed out of town.

This could be the opportunity she needed to determine once and for all whether the bounty hunter's denouncements had some veracity.

Quickly she left the hotel and hustled across the street and down a side alley. She wanted to avoid being seen by any of Fresno's men. Approaching the saloon from the rear, she paused. A surreptitious eye scanned the immediate surroundings to ensure her presence went undetected.

Then, lifting up her skirts, she mounted the back stairs. The door opened on silent hinges. The corridor was empty.

But raised voices drifting up from the saloon below told her that time was not on her side. At any moment, somebody could appear. Even though she was the boss's woman, questions would surely be asked as to her presence in his private domain.

Her fiancé's office was the first on the

left. Fortunately it was unlocked. Gliding into the room, her eyes panned the restricted quarters. This was the first time she had entered this hallowed sanctum.

Outside a dog barked. The discordant yammer sent a tremor of fear scurrying down the girl's spine. The sooner this business was concluded the better.

Over on the far side of the room lay the safe where Fresno was bound to keep all his important papers. But what if it was locked? Any chance of determining the truth would be impossible.

Grasping the handle of the iron safe, she pulled. For the briefest instant it resisted her efforts. A second more insistent tug and it slid open. A sigh of relief escaped from pursed lips as the girl scanned the interior. All manner of documents lay piled up inside tied with official pink ribbons.

Quickly she rifled through them, desperately searching for that all-important paper. She found it at the bottom. The deed of inheritance leaving the Red Dragon saloon and all its appurtenances to one Cody Montaine. Trembling hands gingerly removed the photograph that Lucky Johnson had given her. Laid side by side, she compared the signatures.

Even at this late stage, Felicity entertained the hope that the bounty hunter was wrong.

But there was no doubt.

They were both the same. So he had been telling the truth after all. Lucky Johnson was indeed the real Cody Montaine. And her so-called fiancé? Nought but a charlatan, a chiselling fraudster.

A tear welled up in the young woman's eye. Uncovering the odious deception had left her totally deflated. There was no satisfaction in learning that she had been so callously deceived by the man she had hoped to marry. Her head dropped in despair. The two sheets slipped from her fingers.

'Well now!'

The oily voice cut into the girl's

traumatic distress. So intent had she been to resolve the issue that all else had been pushed aside.

A mile outside the town, Butte Fresno had suddenly realized that he had not locked the safe. Only when he entered the upper corridor of the Red Dragon did the realization strike home that he had an intruder.

Peering round the edge of the open door, it came as a distinct shock to see that it was his betrothed. And she was delving into his private affairs. Dealings that were most assuredly not for the eyes of a potential wife, or anyone else, for that matter.

'What have we here?'

Guilt and shock at being discovered red-handed was written indelibly across the beautiful face. Felicity was totally lost for words. Not waiting for a reply to his query, the trickster quickly stepped into the room and locked the door, thus stymying any hope she might have harboured regarding escape.

'If you wanted to know something in

particular, all you had to do was ask.' His unctuous tones suddenly turned gruff and threatening. 'So what's this all about? Why are you suddenly so interested in the contents of my safe?'

He grabbed hold of the relevant papers and rapidly perused them. Eyes, dark with suspicion, widened.

Now it was Fresno's turn to register surprise. But already his devious mind was reaching the clear and obvious conclusion. An ugly smile creased the hardened features of the blackguard. His head nodded in comprehension. Yet still he was baffled.

'Where did you get this photograph?' he rasped. There was a nervous catch in his voice, the result of identifying the young man depicted in the cracked and faded snapshot. Grasping the girl's arm, he shook her violently. 'Answer me, girl. Who gave you this?'

Felicity cried out in fear and pain. But it was enough to imbue in her the will and tenacity to respond in kind now that the truth was out in the open.

'You're not Cody Montaine,' she hissed struggling ineffectually to wriggle out of the iron grip. 'The real one has told me all about Butte Fresno's attempt to kill him during the war, then steal his identity and inheritance. You'll never get away with it now that I've found out the truth.'

This could only mean that Sergeant Cody Montaine had somehow miraculously survived the shooting and had tracked him down. The realization that his pretence had been rumbled and was under threat came as a bitter pill to swallow. Even now, Montaine could be planning his revenge close at hand. And if he and the girl knew the truth, who else was there?

Fresno knew that his days in Las Vegas could be numbered if he didn't act fast. But the scheming trickster was no easy pushover. And he suddenly realized that he had an ace in the hole.

The photograph!

And it was clearly the original. Even

if copies existed, they would lack any authenticity.

Destroy that and he was in the clear. Then all he had to do was get rid of the girl and that meddling death cheater.

A mirthless laugh, shot through with spine-tingling menace, issued from between the thin mean lips. His next words were punched out in a low yet chilling whisper.

'Do you honestly suppose that I could allow you or that interfering skunk to expose my brilliant charade? I've built up a sizeable empire around here. And nobody is gonna take it from me.' The twisted features leered at the terrified girl. He clicked his tongue in mocking admonition. 'A fiancée who just couldn't keep her purty little nose out of the trough. Well you know what curiosity did to the poor old cat, don't you my dear?'

Felicity shuddered. Fear, intermingled with loathing, suffused her whole being. She tried to shrink away from this man to whom she had so unashamedly plied her troth. How could she have been such a fool to have been thus deluded, smitten by such a fraud?

The girl was not given any further time to reflect on her naive deception. Fresno's charade had been exposed along with the fraudster's ruthless streak. With everything out in the open, he reverted to his unfeigned character. An ugly growl issued from between clenched teeth as he struck a match and applied it to the photograph.

Seeing the all-important evidence about to disappear in a pile of ash, she lunged at the raised arm. The sudden counterblow took Fresno by surprise. He grappled with the writhing creature as she desperately tried to retrieve the photograph. But all to no avail.

A sharp right-hander cracked against her jaw. Blackness enfolded Felicity in its dark embrace. Silently she fell to the floor, unconscious.

But the unexpected fracas had unleashed dire and unforeseen consequences.

A flailing arm had displaced a lamp

which crashed to the floor, oil spilling from the shattered glass bowl. Flames instantly took hold. Greedly, they licked at the saturated carpet spreading like a rampant plague across the floor. Fresno grabbed a cushion and tried to douse the lethal blaze. But it was a hopeless task.

Desperation was reflected in the cheating desperado's haunted gaze. In a matter of seconds, his dreams of power and affluence were being consumed before his very eyes.

Faced with such a catastrophe, there was only one course of action open to him. A gleam of inspiration was mirrored in the fraudster's manic gaze.

'And you, Miss interfering Harper, are gonna be my insurance policy.'

13

. . . Into The Fire

Cody had likewise come to a decision. Back at his secret campsite, he coaxed the embers of a fire back from the dead. Coffee was brewed. A mug laced with a generous slug of whiskey helped to curb his restlessness.

But having to wait around until nightfall in the hope that Felicity would come up with the goods did not sit well. Never known for being the most patient of men, he was chafing at the bit. Things needed pushing along. Eight years of searching now counted for nothing.

The time for a showdown was now. Leave it any longer and Fresno might well gain the upper hand. The resolution made, Cody doused the camp-fire and headed back for Las Vegas at a fast lick.

Smoke rising in the static air caught his attention while still a mile outside the town, an ominous warning sign according to that itch nagging at the back of his neck. He slapped the leathers, urging the grey to a faster pace. Pounding hoofs beat a rhythmic cadence on the hard-packed earth as he entered the main street.

Once again, Cody's hunch had not failed him.

Wrestling the charging beast to a grinding halt, he leapt from the saddle just as the town's fire brigade arrived. Onlookers gazed awestruck at the rapidly spreading inferno.

Fire was one of the worst catastrophes faced by all frontier settlements. The predominantly wooden buildings stood little chance of survival once the flames had taken a firm hold in the hot dry atmosphere. Only a flash storm stood any hope of snuffing out the conflagration. And on this day, the sky was cloudless.

Nevertheless, the urgent orders issued

by the fire chief might help to save some of the buildings.

'What happened here?' Cody inquired of the Red Dragon's gaping bartender who had joined the morbid fire-watchers. It was his job going up in smoke. Even so, the guy just stood there, rooted to the spot, transfixed.

Although lethal, fire always exercised a mesmeric attraction, even for those intimately affected. A line of bucket-carriers had been organized to help control the rapidly escalating blaze. They had their work cut out.

'Nobody seems to know,' replied the ogling 'keep. 'The boss, Mr Montaine, left town a couple of hours since.' Cody shivered as the Grim Reaper's scythe tickled his backbone on hearing his own name mentioned. He felt like a ghost attending his own funeral. 'Then before you know it, he was back. Reckoned he'd forgotten some'n. The next thing I know, smoke comes pouring through the ceiling boards.'

'Is he in there now?'

'Ain't seen hide nor hair of him since then. Far as I know everyone got out once the flames took a hold.' Morrison shook his head slowly, shock registering on the blotched features.

At that moment, there was a rending crash as the saloon's roof disintegrated. Sparks flew into the air. Anybody left inside hadn't got a hope in Hades of surviving.

Nursing a heavy heart, Cody left the gaping barman and headed down the street to the hotel where Felicity was staying. He issued a silent prayer that she would be installed in her room.

Nobody was in the lobby. The discordant clamour of a vigorously rung bell brought forth no scurrying receptionist. Ogling the fire, no doubt. Taking the stairs three at a time, Cody soon established that the girl was also absent.

Panic tightened its insidious hold on his guts.

Where could she be? Back on the main street, he took a direct course down an alley opposite to gain the rear of the saloon. What if Felicity had been trapped inside when the fire broke out?

The notion made him quake with dread. The fire had spread to the buildings on either side of the saloon. The fact that his inheritance was disappearing before his very eyes was of little consequence to the implacable vigilante. All he could think of was establishing that the delectable Miss Harper was safe and well.

Eyes straining to penetrate the hazy clouds of smoke billowing from the saloon, his eye suddenly caught a bright splash of green and blue on the ground at the foot of the back stairs. He grabbed hold of the clump of feathers, instantly recognizing them as belonging to that ridiculous hat Felicity had been wearing when they last spoke.

Could that mean she had escaped? If so, where was she now?

Clearly the girl had come to the saloon with the intention of verifying the story he had related. She would not have purposefully left the hat unless

. . . Fresno had caught her in the act.

The more he thought about it, the greater became his fear that the girl had been abducted by his hated adversary. Searching around, he soon came across more evidence to support his theory. Bending down he picked up a single lady's shoe. Now he was certain that Felicity was in the odious hands of Butte Fresno. And she appeared to have been roughly manhandled. But at least she must still be alive.

So where could the rat have taken her?

Only one other person was likely to have the answer to that conundrum.

Sheriff Mingus Charlie Brucker.

With no further time to waste, Cody hurried round to the main street and leapt on to his horse. In a flurry of dust, heels digging and leathers slapping, he urged the grey to a furious gallop. Nobody paid him any mind. All eyes were fastened on to the furious activities of the firefighters.

'You varmints best let me out of here.'
The angry voice, muted yet edged with
more than a trace of alarm, came from
the tackle shed adjoining the barn of
the Box Bar M. 'Otherwise you're both
goin' down for a long spell in the
slammer. And I'll make sure the
governor throws away the key.'

Howard Mason and his son had
established temporary quarters in the
only building to survive the attack on
the ranch. They had buried old Jethro
in a hallowed spot adjacent to the
rancher's wife.

'It's twenty years minimum with no
parole for holdin' a lawman against his
will,' continued the weasel-faced Brucker.
'But I could ask the judge to go easy on
yuh both if'n you let me out now.'

When Cal Mason had arrived back
with the lawman, ostensibly to investigate the murderous attack, his father
had been waiting with a loaded
shotgun. Brucker had been too stunned

215

to put up much resistance to his own apprehension and imprisonment.

Now he was venting his spleen.

Both men were under no illusions that incarcerating an official of the law, no matter how dubious his credentials, was next door to a hanging offence. Their fate was now firmly in the hands of the mysterious bounty hunter. Unless he substantiated his claim against the bogus Cody Montaine, they would be well and truly up Cripple Creek without a canoe, let alone a paddle.

'If'n that skunk don't shut his trap, I'll do it for him,' railed Cal Mason clenching his fist. He was moving towards the lean-to when a pounding of hoofs echoed across the dusty corral.

'It's Cody!' announced the young man hurrying across to meet the bustling rider. 'And just in time to save this jasper's mangy hide.'

Vaulting out of the saddle, Cody spluttered bluntly, 'Where's Brucker?'

'Over in the tackle shed,' replied Cal.

'Then get him out here fast.'

Cal could see that his old partner was fired up and in no mood for lengthy explanations. Without another word, Cal hustled over to the shed. Gun drawn and cocked, he unbolted the door and called out to the occupant.

'All right, Sheriff,' came the deliberately meek utterance, 'Come on out. Guess you got us by the short and curlies.'

'And about time too,' huffed Brucker emerging from the gloomy interior. 'But don't think by settin' me loose, you can get away with this. I intend seein' that you both get sent down for a — '

The seedy lawdog never got to finish his turbid rant.

There, standing before him, was a third man. And he was pointing a pistol at his guts. Cal Mason couldn't resist a harsh guffaw.

A leery smirk rested on the face of the newcomer.

'Howdie there, Mingus,' said the tall stranger in a cheery voice that belied a hint of the sardonic. 'Remember me?'

Charlie Brucker scowled. 'What's goin' on here? I don't know you. Never seen you afore.'

Cody stroked his chin in thought. 'Now let me see. When was it?' He paused as if dredging up some long distant memory. 'Yeh, I recall now.' A gimlet eye fastened on to the baffled sheriff. Then he spat out the venomous retort. 'Don't tell me you've fogotten what happened on . . . Epitaph Ridge?'

For a brief second, Brucker's skeletal face remained one of confused bewilderment. Then it all came flooding back. How could he possibly forget shooting down a man and leaving him for dead.

'Montaine!'

'That's right, Mingus.' The hard features of the risen corpse cracked in a grim smile. 'I've come back from the dead to haunt you and that bastard who stole my life. Idaho Black is stoking the fiery furnace, and so will you if'n I don't get some answers.' Cody stepped forward and grabbed the quivering weasel by the throat, his gun jabbing into the varmint's belly. 'You all set to let me know where he's holed up?'

Stunned into silence by this bolt from the blue, Charlie Brucker could only stand and stare. A harsh backhander from his old sergeant brought him back to the here and now.

'Fresno has reached the end of the line, Charlie,' snapped the bounty hunter. 'His days are numbered. The Red Dragon has gone up in smoke and he's fled taking a hostage with him. Miss Harper uncovered his dubious dealings and discovered how he'd wormed his way into my identity. Now he's scarpered and I want to know where he's gone.'

'That weren't none of my doing,' blurted out the cowering rat. 'I've tried to go straight by upholding the law in Las Vegas.'

A harsh laugh all round greeted this announcement.

'Don't give me that, Brucker,' rapped

Howard Mason. 'You're in this up to your neck.'

'And the only way out for you, mister,' interjected Cody, emphasizing his threat by jamming the pistol up the guy's twitching snout, 'is by spilling the beans. Now where has Fresno gone?'

Sensing he had an edge, Brucker gave the demand a noncommital shrug. 'Butte kept all his dealings secret. None of us knew what he was up to. We were just the hired hands.'

Cody knew the varmint was prevaricating, playing for time. And time was not on the hunter's side. Every second squandered meant that Fresno was getting further away. He, therefore, came to the abrupt conclusion that the time for lengthy verbal persuasion was at an end.

Arriving in a flurry of dust, Cody had nevertheless observed that the Masons had been passing the time branding young calves.

'Pass me one of them irons.' The blunt order was addressed to Cal

Mason. Hand held out, Cody's steely gaze never left his quarry.

Cal hesitated. 'You sure about this, Cody?'

'Just do it,' came back the blunt demand.

The red hot iron was placed into his gloved hand.

'Now talk, you son of Satan,' he hissed wagging the steaming iron, 'else feel the wrath of your master.'

Brucker's eyes widened. Pure terror wrinkled the seamed contours of his angular visage as the sizzling red metal drew closer. The searing heat scorched the weasel's eyebrows.

14

End Game

Ten minutes later, Cody Montaine was galloping across the rolling plains of the Gallinas. A sharp stab of the lethal branding iron into the wall of the barn inches from Mingus Charlie's head was enough to open the floodgates.

Fresno had secreted all the booty he had made at a hideout in the Sangre de Cristos. He and Charlie Brucker had come across the abandoned miner's cabin by accident one day after straying into a box canyon. Penasco Gulch was the perfect stash for all their ill-gotten gains. That way, no questions could be posed by nosy bankers or government auditors.

Brucker was under no illusion that his old buddy had intended skipping the territory leaving him to carry the can. His outpouring was vitriolic.

A quick discussion regarding the best means of reaching Penasco Gulch elicited the finding that going through Buckskin Gap would save a half day. If he rode all night and the following day, Cody surmised that he could reach the hidden stash ahead of his antagonist.

The ride was hard and exhausting.

Subsisting on pure adrenalin, he stopped only to rest his mount and for calls of nature. The thought of the delectable Miss Harper in the clutches of his hated foe drove him on relentlessly. After eight long years, he had no intention of being thwarted in his endeavour at the last hurdle.

Finally, the carved rock known as Mexican Hat came into view. The hidden canyon lay just beyond.

Tethering his horse out of sight in a clump of pine trees, he quickly investigated the inner recess to determine whether Fresno had arrived. Cody gave thanks to his Maker that the Gulch was unoccupied. Quickly, he climbed the fractured edge of the mesa. From there he would have a panoramic view of all approaches to the hideout.

He did not have long to wait.

A deep sigh of relief hissed from tightly clenched teeth as a low cloud of dust rose from the plains. It could only have originated from a horse-drawn wagon. Five minutes later, the distinct form of a flat-bed driven by two horses hove into view.

Cody stood up for a better look.

Fresno was sitting on the bench seat. A whip clutched in his right hand flicked at the horses, directing them towards the apparent solid rock wall ahead. In the bed of the wagon lying on a rough smelly horse blanket, Felicity Harper lay bound and gagged.

'Whooaah there, you mangey nags,' hollered Fresno, hauling back on the leathers. The wagon lurched to a grinding halt.

The brigand stared up at the mesa. Rubbing the grit from his eyes, he tried to refocus. A frown creased the ribbed forehead. He felt sure that he had seen what looked like a man atop the rocky excrescence. But there was nothing there now. He shrugged. It must have been a desert mirage. His eyes were playing tricks.

And was it any wonder after the traumatic events of the last few days.

This damned Harper woman was proving to be a handful he regretted having brought along. What in thunder had made him propose to her? She had a sharp tongue that a few brisk slaps had failed to curb. A gag had been the only means of staying the incessant harangue.

He cast a waspish eye at the tethered girl. Maybe he should get rid of her now. Toying with the gun on his hip, he discarded the notion.

She might still prove useful as a bargaining tool should his plans for escape over the border into Colorado hit the skids. After all, the girl was the daughter of a leading congressman in St Louis. The old boy would pay a goodly ransom to have his only child returned in one piece.

Whipping up the horses, he moved towards the concealed entrance to the canyon. Beyond the sheltering screen of trees, there was just enough room to allow the passage of a horse-drawn wagon. Even so, the wheels scraped alarmingly against the protruding rocks. But at last, it thankfully trundled into the enclosed arena, at the far end of which lay the old cabin.

The sun beat down, turning the enclosed tract into a sweltering cauldron. Rippling heat waves scurried across the tumbled blocks of orange sandstone. For an instant, Fresno once again thought he saw a figure standing atop the rimrock; a black silhouette against the bright blue of the clear sky.

He blinked once. And the chimera was gone — another illusion created by the incessant heat. The sooner he and the girl were away from this barren wilderness, the better. All that he needed to do now was to load up the wagon with the hidden loot and disappear into the wide blue yonder. A new name and a new beginning beckoned invitingly.

Smiling to himself, Fresno stepped down from the wagon. It didn't take more than three trips to load up the trunks full of gold nuggets and American dollar bills.

The girl's eyes blazed with unconcealed hate. Her rampant animosity had had no effect on the blackguard.

'Just think on it, girl,' scoffed Fresno. 'If you hadn't been so nosy, I might have been tempted to marry you after all. Then all this,' a lazy hand indicated the vast wealth, 'could have been your'n. Too late now. Although you're still worth a pretty penny as hostage bait. I'm certain that the doting father will pay heavily to get his daughter back safe and sound. So it's best that you don't rile my patience.' He slammed a bunched fist into the palm of his hand. 'It wouldn't be right to deliver up damaged goods, now would it?'

Fresno burst into a paroxysm of acrid laughter as he mounted the stoop and leathered the team back into motion.

Re-negotiating the narrow entrance to the hidden canyon required extra care. The heavy load made it far more unwieldy. Twice it stuck. And only the urgent encouragement of the whip gave added impetus to the terrified horses.

Then —

Something landed with a hard thump on the back of the wagon.

* * *

Cody had witnessed the whole episode in the hidden arena but was prevented from intervening by the close proximity of the pinioned captive. All he could do was watch and wait, trusting that a suitable opportunity to turn the tables on the bastard would present itself.

The narrow ravine was the ideal location. Carefully dropping down between the stands of fractured rock, he managed to find a ledge overlooking the entrance that was no more than six feet above where the wagon would pass. And there he waited. Holding his breath, tension strained his nerves to breaking point. As the wagon rumbled beneath the ledge, he jumped.

An arm snaked around the neck of the driver. Taken by surprise, Fresno dropped the whip. Panicked by the unexpected jolt, the horses bolted. Smashing through the screen of pine trees, the attacker was forced to release his grip.

Fresno was no easy hit and took advantage of the situation. A swinging fist slammed into the side of Cody's head rocking him back. Instinctively he grabbed for the brake lever with both hands. It was his salvation. Leaning half out of the wagon, he managed to kick out. His right boot connected with Fresno's chest eliciting a pained grunt and forcing the kidnapper to pull back out of reach.

The brief respite enabled Cody to shake off the numbing effect of the jolt.

Scrambling onto the seat, he despatched a couple of lethal jabs at his enemy's face. Blood spouted from a burst nose. Fresno was forced to release the reins, losing control of the wagon, which careered onward unchecked.

Bouncing and jerking about, the two adversaries struggled to attain an advantage. No easy feat atop a wagon heading for oblivion. Desperation drove Butte Fresno to release his hold on the seat backrest. Both hands fastened on to the bounty hunter's neck. Thumbs dug deep into Cody's windpipe. A lurid growl of triumph hissed from Fresno's twisted maw as the kidnapper pressed home his advantage.

The tethered prisoner could only stare impotently, willing her paladin to somehow break the lethal grip. But to no avail. Grinding teeth warped in a bitter grin of victory as Fresno sensed his opponent weakening.

Fresno loomed over his victim. A feral sound akin to that of a wild animal rumbled in his throat as he pressed home his advantage.

'Grrrrrrrrgh!'

Cody's eyes bulged; his face assumed a purple hue. All efforts to break the fatal grip proved ineffectual.

Was this how it was going to end?

Blackness flooded his blood-starved brain.

But fate was about to step in and tip the balance in Cody Montaine's favour. Wildly careering at full pelt and totally out of control, it was only a matter of time before the runaway wagon came to a sticky end.

And it was a large boulder that came to his rescue.

Without any warning, the wagon lurched into the air. Its front wheel broke up in myriad pieces. Both combatants were thrown clear. Arms and legs flailing, they grovelled in the dust, struggling to shake off the stupefying potency of the brutal collision.

Fresno was the first to stumble to his feet. Head bowed, his opponent was still suffering the effects of the savage throttling.

The blackguard grabbed for his pistol.

'I should have checked you were dead on the battlefield, Montaine,' he rasped, spitting out a mouthful of sand. 'My mistake. But I won't make another.' The gun rose, the click of the hammer echoing across the desert plain.

Cody was still on his knees when a deep-throated roar shattered the tension. Fresno reeled drunkenly. A large patch of red blossomed on his chest. A look of utter confusion was written across his ashen face. Stumbling backwards, his legs turned to jelly. Then he pitched over and lay still, his body splayed across a clump of cholla cactus.

Cody lurched to his feet, little better than his adversary, apart from the fact that some miracle had occurred to keep him in the land of the living.

The gentle trot of hoofs penetrated his befuddled brain. Soon after, a strong arm was supporting his battered frame. And through the blurred haze, a dark figure emerged.

'Reckoned you might need some backup,' enunciated the welcome tones of Cal Mason. Cody forced his ravaged features into a semblance of a smile. Never had he been more grateful for another person's intervention. 'Seems like I arrived in the nick of time.'

A muffled cry found both men looking towards the remnants of the smashed wagon. They hurried over and helped Felicity Harper out from beneath a welter of splintered wood and bent metal. Luckily, she was unhurt. The gag and bindings were quickly removed.

Instantly, the girl fell into the arms of her saviour. He held her close, a loose smile playing across the pale features.

'How could I have been such a gullible fool?' she intoned, her head buried in the shoulder of the tall bounty hunter. 'Will you ever forgive me?' She raised her pale face, gazing at the man who had saved her.

'Does that mean . . . ?' mumbled a still rather stunned Cody Montaine.

'What do you think?' came the somewhat coy interjection.

Cody closed his eyes, satisfied. His revenge was complete, and with it had come an added bonus.

THE END